I0735452

DEATH & PESTILENCE

A Horror Anthology

sands press
Brockville, Ontario

DEATH & PESTILENCE

A Horror Anthology

sands press

sands press

A division of 10361976 Canada Inc.
300 Central Avenue West
Brockville, Ontario
K6V 5V2

Toll Free 1-800-563-0911 or 613-345-2687
http://www.sandspress.com

ISBN 978-1-988281-14-8

Cover Concept by Kristine Barker & Renee Hare
Formatting by Kevin Davidson, Renee Hare
Publisher Sands Press

1st Printing March 2017

To book an author for your live event, please call: 1-800-563-0911

Sands Press is a literary publisher interested in new and established authors wishing to develop and market their product. For more information please visit our website at www.sandspress.com.

Andrea Johnson

Andrea Johnson was born in Kitchener, ON and earned her BA in History from the University of Waterloo and BEd from Western University. Andrea taught secondary level History, English, and Religious Studies for ten years in Waterloo, London and Kingston, ON. Andrea now works at Queen's School of Business as an Application Advisor for professional graduate business programs. Along with being a self-professed Anglophile, Andrea is a voracious reader and loves nothing more than getting lost in the world of fiction.

Anita Vandeneykel

Her love for story telling began at a very young age by writing and performing plays for her family, so it was no surprise that Anita Vandeneykel choose a career in the arts. At 21 this young actress made the bold move from Maple Ridge, BC to Toronto where she performed in theatre, television and film. It was during this time that Anita realized it was the story telling aspect of performing that she loved. She took control of her journey by writing, producing and performing plays and short films. Anita studied screen writing at George Brown College in Toronto and through Blake Snyder's Institute in Los Angeles. She has retired from performing however writing is still a focus for her and she is always listening to, reading or watching a great story.

Shannon Johnson

What I enjoy most about reading is plummeting into the realms the author has created readers. I like to broaden my horizons and read outside of my comfort level.

Leisa Price-Storey

An avid reader and freelance writer/editor, I've worked at a bookstore, newspaper and currently work in a library. In my personal library, I'm proud to display some books that I've edited. Editing manuscripts is both challenging and rewarding. I enjoy working with Sands Press to help authors fulfill their dreams.

Kevin Davidson

Death & Pestilence was the final book that Kevin worked on before he became ill. Sadly, Kevin passed away in November of 2016. He was the driving force behind the design and vision of Sands Press, and every book published up to this point has Kevin's vision as their template. Kevin was a loved and valued co-worker and friend, and is missed dearly.

Authors List

1st Place B.G. Strong

2nd Place E. J. Walker

3rd Place Guy Cheston

4th/5th Place TIE Caito Caol & Dennis Stein

Runners Up

Flynn Gray

Rob Powell

Stephen Kriedemann

Micky Neilson

Victoria Griffen

Chevoque

Andrea Merchak

Michaela Turcotte

Nathan S. M. Knapp

Rod Martinez

J. P. Frost

Rick Weiss

Jasmine Love

Paul Pickett

Jay Michael Wright II

Sands Press wishes to thank all the talented writers who participated in this project, without whom this anthology wouldn't have been possible.

Presenting...

First Place Winner
Brystan (B.G.) Strong

Brystan Strong (also known as B.G. Strong) is a native Oregonian with her BA in Creative Writing and her Masters in Library Information Science. She enjoys writing darker short fiction, but has published a children's book which is available on Amazon. She lives in Southern Oregon with her significant other, and her pets: a cat, a bird, and a fish.

Author website: www.bgstrong.com

Plague //

BRYSTAN (B. G.) STRONG

The whole world smelled like sour milk. For most people, it didn't bother them. They had gotten used to it, or had forgotten what the world smelled like before. But me, I'm sensitive to this kind of thing. And I'll never forget what it was like before.

I was seven years old when I lost my eyes. I was one of the first infected in my district and somehow I'm still alive. The pain was excruciating. It started out as just an irritation, as if there was dust in my eyes. Then, it turned into a burning, followed by swelling, pus, and oh-my-god the smell; a sour yet burning smell. One wouldn't think that your eyes could smell like anything, but when they are rotting inside of their sockets, that's a different story.

I took them out myself, my eyes. With a spoon. The pain was unbearable so I just scooped them out. I had looked for a grapefruit spoon, but in the heat of the moment I decided on a teaspoon. It horrified my mother. I had never heard her scream so loud. The whole world screams now.

I listened to the news on the television. There isn't much else to do anymore. The plague had wiped out the desire for entertainment. We just clung to the news, to religion. Some of us just wanted to wallow.

On the news they were talking about the body tunnels. You see, there was so much death in the world that the cemeteries were too full. They buried the bodies four, five, sometimes six deep. Now they were tunneling under buildings: businesses, homes, schools and churches. Caverns full of the dead. While you eat your dinner above ground, your loved ones could be rotting right underneath your dining room floor. We weren't much different from the corpses that would be below us though. Since the plague hit, we were all just rotting flesh.

The news anchor coughed. She had only been at the news station a week. She'll be dead by next week.

I heard the door open. A slow, light creaking. Mother was home. She sat next to me on the couch and grabbed my hand. I grabbed her other hand. The four fingers on her left hand and the three on her right were thin and cold. My mother has been lucky. The doctors have been able to cut out the plague, but I had to wonder what would happen when she lost all her fingers. Where would they cut next?

"What did the doctors say?" I asked.

"They think they can slow it down by removing his leg, but they don't know for how long," she said.

"I understand," I said. I used to say "I see", but puns just aren't funny when the whole world is dying.

"Can I watch my show?" Mother asked. I nodded and motioned in the direction of the television.

Mother was someone who found and then clung to religion to help her cope. I didn't much care for it. I didn't believe in God. What God would let this happen? The only thing I believed in anymore was death. Death appeared every day. I didn't have to see it anymore to know it was real. Death is my faith.

The man on the television, a preacher of sorts, did a lot of yelling. He said that it was humanity's sin that had caused the plague to come. People had given up alcohol, fatty foods, meat, sex, and yet the plague was still here. Today he yelled about the apocalypse. He spoke of the four horsemen: conquest, war, famine, and death. Now we had to prepare for the end times, and live our lives in hope that God would save us.

I didn't hope. It's hard to have hope when there is nothing to hope for. My mother, on the other hand, had a lot of hope for some reason. I guess all mothers do.

I could only handle the yelling man on the television for so long before my head started to hurt. I decided to go to my room to lay down. My room was hot and stuffy. I wanted nothing more than to open the window. But, as everyone knew, that's how you let the plague in. Plus, there hadn't been any fresh air in years. If I wanted to feel a breeze, I had to turn my fan on.

I remember when there used to be fresh air. I have memories of playing outside as a toddler, and my dress moving in the wind. I had a lot of dresses, in a rainbow of colors. My hair was softer then, and shone bright like the sun. I was plump, and my skin pink and healthy. I remember my mother sitting underneath our old maple tree, knitting booties for my then baby brother. The booties were baby blue, they matched my mother's eyes. That felt like a hundred years ago. My childhood got yanked out from under me when the plague came. No more dresses, no more color, and most of my hair was now in clumps on the bottom of the bathtub. I never knew if she finished the booties.

It came so fast. It started in Africa. We weren't scared then. Africa was distant, underdeveloped, and poor. Of course they would get it. But then it spread like wildfire, across the oceans and in all the continents. When we started to feel scared, it was too late. We were already dead.

At first, they had a lot of names for it: bird flu, swine flu, AIDS, malaria, bubonic plague, and leprosy. But it wasn't any of those things. It was worse, and the media decided to just refer to it as Plague II. Plague II had killed everyone I ever knew and loved. Except of course my mother and my brother, but it was only a matter of time.

Dinner was early because mother felt tired. She grew more and more tired every day. As mother said grace, I wondered who they would bury under our house. Dinner was some sort of protein shake and water. I could hardly call it 'dinner'. It was cold, and it never made me feel full, it just made me feel less hungry. Most of the real food was gone. Now, the government dropped off buckets of water and bland powdery substance for us to live on. Natural crops died out long ago, and even though people said Twinkies would last forever, I had never seen one.

Mother went to bed right after dinner, complaining of severe pain in her hands and fatigue. She would have to get up early tomorrow to see my brother at the hospital. I went to bed, too. I didn't sleep well anymore. It's difficult to know if it's time to go to bed when you don't know when the sun sets. But even so, after a while, I fell asleep.

I awoke to a cold chill. A breeze? And a smell of something sweet and smoky. Like incense. Not the sour smell that permeated the earth.

"Is someone there?" I asked.

"Yes," said the voice. The voice was both masculine and feminine, soft and loud, close and distant. It was unlike anything I had ever heard before.

"Who are you?" I asked.

"You know who I am," It said. I felt the voice inside my chest, in my head, and all around me.

"Death," I said. "You're real."

"You always knew that," It said.

"Yes. I suppose. Does that mean God is real? And Heaven? Hell?"

"I can't tell you that," Death said. "I am only this one thing."

It was closer now.

"You've come for me," I said.

"No."

"My brother? He's at the hospital."

"No."

"My Mother?" I asked. Death didn't answer. "But how? She's been well."

"I come when the time is right. Not when you expect it."

"And my brother?"

"Soon."

"And," the words stuck in my throat. "And me?"

"I come for everyone, at some point."

"What do I do?" I asked. "How do I live without her? And what will happen to my brother?"

"Say your goodbyes," Death said, and the presence vanished.

I went to my mother's room and curled up next to her in her bed, like I used to as a small child. I held her hand, kissed her cheek and told her that I loved her.

I placed my head on her chest, and listened to her heart.

Thump-thump

A sweet, smoky smell filled the room.

Thump-thump

"I'll miss you," I said.

Thump-thump

"I'll try to take care of my brother, as best as I can."

Thump-thump

"Goodbye."

The smell left the room, and I knew she was gone. I left my mother's room and went back to my own. I faced my window and opened it. The whole world smelled like sour milk. It wasn't as strong as it used to be. I was starting to get used to it.

Runner Up

Flynn Gray

Flynn Gray writes horror and dark fantasy fiction, loves books & drinks too much coffee. To learn more about her work please visit her at:

http://www.flynngray.wordpress.com

http://www.facebook.com/FlynnGrayWriter

The Curse of Greenwater Falls

FLYNN GRAY

September 23, 1987, 12:07 a.m. Route 64, Greenwater Falls County.

The woman had appeared in the path of his headlights far too quickly for him to have a chance to react. He saw a flash of the wide-eyed panic on her dirty, blood-streaked face before impact sent her body sailing into the air. His foot was still crushing the brake pedal into the floor for what seemed like an eternity after the car had skidded to a stop, eyes frozen on streaks of blood and flesh that slid down the cracked windscreen millimeter by painful millimeter.

Panic threatened to creep up his throat and suffocate him, as Jake placed the car into park and pulled the handbrake up, running on automatic pilot as he turned off the ignition and the lights. No, not the lights, too dark now. He flipped the lights back on, noting a little hysterically that he'd have a dead battery to deal with later, as if that mattered now. Hesitantly, he slid out of the car.

There were dark, shiny smears and splotches on the road around the car, reflecting dully in the dim lighting, and he turned away quickly to open the Chevelle's rear door and fumble around for the flashlight he knew was rolling around in there somewhere on the back floor.

His hand closed around the familiar shape and he switched it on, shaking it a few times in a futile attempt to make the feeble beam stronger. Taking a deep breath, he closed the car door and turned the narrow beam of light towards the road.

He followed the grisly trail of smears and splatters back about a dozen feet, until the flashlight picked out the shape of a large, disfigured lump of flesh and bone lying at the edge of the highway. At the sight and smell, Jake's knees finally gave out, along with his stomach, and he collapsed and vomited violently in the middle of the road.

Gathering his fortitude once more, he stumbled to his feet again and slowly approached the bloody mass, needing to face what he had done. As he drew closer, however, he realized that something was horribly wrong.

Even as mangled as it was, the corpse was clearly not human. The shape was completely wrong; there was far too much fur and...antlers? Jake fell back, collapsing onto the road with relief, too relieved to even care that he was sitting in a large puddle of blood that was steadily seeping into his jeans. It was just a small deer, not a woman. He hadn't killed anyone.

Pushing the vision of the woman's face from his mind, he pulled himself to his feet and began moving back towards his car. It had obviously been some kind of hallucination brought on by too much coffee and a lack of sleep. There had never been any woman.

He hadn't taken two steps before the Chevelle's engine roared to life, seemingly of its own volition, brake lights flashing briefly before the car was placed into gear and began roaring away, leaving Jake alone in the dark with the corpse of the deer and his flickering flashlight.

"Hey!" Jake began running after his car foolishly, waving his arms and his flashlight wildly, before he realized the futility and gave up as the taillights disappeared around a bend in the road.

It was at this point, as he was standing completely alone in the middle of a deserted highway at just past midnight, that his flashlight decided to go out completely.

"Great, just great," he muttered, tossing it away to the side of the road.

Running his hands through his hair, he struggled to comprehend what had just happened. Who had stolen his car? He hadn't passed any other traffic since the last town, over 50 miles ago. There was nothing but dense forest on either side of the road, and he had no idea how far away the nearest town, or even house, might be. Though there must have been someone else out here, lurking in the darkness, waiting for the best moment to take his car. He shivered a little and looked around, but the darkness was absolute on that cool, moonless night. Who knew what was out there?

He listened carefully for any suspicious noises but it was eerily silent, the whole forest perfectly still as though in anticipation. Deciding to take a chance, Jake started walking in the direction that he had been driving. Maybe he would get lucky and find a house, or even a town. Anything was better than standing alone in the pitch dark wondering who or what else might be watching him from the shadows. He stumbled along doggedly, only able to tell if he'd wandered off the road if there was a change in the texture of the terrain beneath his feet.

With his concentration entirely devoted to remaining on the road and not tripping over his own shoes in the disorienting darkness, it took a few moments for Jake to realize that he could hear the sound of a car engine approaching rapidly from the direction he was heading. His spirits lifted as he saw the glow of headlights brightening the night sky ahead of him.

The car came into view, high beams striking Jake blind as he began waving his arms in an attempt to flag the car down. He was so relieved to find some sign of humanity, of release from the unrelenting darkness, that he didn't even consider that this car might bring his final doom rather than deliverance. He didn't realize until far too late that the car was accelerating directly at him, and he didn't even recognize his own car until it was mere inches away from his frozen body.

The brutal impact sent him crashing over the hood and into the windscreen, and the last thing he saw was the terrified, bloodied face of the woman behind the wheel, the woman who had run in front of his car earlier that night.

*****

September 23, 1987, 8:54 a.m. Route 64, Greenwater Falls County.

Sargent John McAllister had been in charge of the small crew of police officers that maintained law and order in Greenwater Falls County for over a decade. When the expected call came in around 7 a.m., he'd called in the only other officer on duty, a newbie of only six months on the force by the name of Brooks, and headed out to the scene.

And it was always the same scene. McAllister stood back and had a cigarette with the driver of the logging truck who had called it in, watching Brooks carefully pull on the blue disposable gloves and start checking the corpse and the car's glovebox for ID and registration.

"Driver's license says this guy's name is Jake Webber," Brooks called back over his shoulder. "Registration is in the same name."

McAllister stubbed out the cigarette under the toe of his boot. "Okay then, take down the details and you can write up the accident report when we get back to the station."

"Accident? Are you sure, Sarge?"

"Yep. There's that deer corpse back there, and the car obviously hit something, so it must've hit that deer and Mr. Webber was critically injured in the impact. Open and shut."

"But his injuries are far too extensive to be caused by that kind of accident. He looks like he was beaten to a pulp. And why is the car so far from the deer? It's at least a 100 meters back, maybe more."

"It's a good, reasonable explanation kid. Let's go."

"I don't think it's that simple, Sarge. We need crime scene specialists out here."

McAllister sighed. Why'd he have to get stuck with a persistent idealist this year? None of the others ever looked that close or gave a damn. The less paperwork, the better.

"Kid, you ever wonder why I've been stuck as a Sargent out in the back wood pips for the past twelve years? It ain't because I like it out here that much. Hell, the place grows on you after a while, but you don't want to get stuck out here for good with zero career prospects. Take my word on this one Brooks, write up the accident report, sign off on it, and don't rock the damn boat. It ain't worth it."

"But..."

McAllister cut him off. "Whatever goes on out here has been going on since the horse an' buggy days, and it ain't going to stop any time soon. It was here long before us and will still be here long after we're gone."

"The curse." The old trucker nodded sagely, crossing himself as he glanced around at the woods.

"Curse?" Brooks' voice had increased an octave.

"Every Autumn equinox," the trucker replied. "If there's someone out and about on the roads around Greenwater Falls on that night, it takes 'em."

"You are joking, right? This is some newbie initiation thing?"

McAllister couldn't blame Brooks for his incredulous tone. He had the exact same attitude the first time the locals warned him. When the first body had shown up just like this one during his first Autumn stationed here. When he had kicked up a fuss and called in the big gun detectives from the city, and had been reprimanded for wasting police resources for his trouble.

"Look, kid, you don't have to believe us, but I'm in charge here and you'll damn well write up what I tell you to and leave it at that. It's for your own good. And if you're still stuck out here in a year's time, we'll see if maybe you don't think again."

He ignored Brooks' mutinous look and slid back into the cruiser. The coroner and tow truck had arrived and it was time to get out of their way and let them do their job.

*****

Greenwater Falls Morning Herald, September 24, 1987, p. 3.

24-year-old Jake Webber was discovered dead in his car, a 1971 Chevrolet Chevelle, in the early hours of yesterday morning.

Mr. Webber appeared to have suffered severe physical trauma, which has been ruled as the cause of death. The source of his injuries has been reported in a statement released by Greenwater Falls County Police Department as a result of a car accident. According to police, Mr. Webber's vehicle also displayed significant signs of damage, consistent with a collision with a deer, the body of which was also found some distance away from Mr. Webber's car.

Police have declined to comment further on the similarity of Mr. Webber's death to that of young Canadian tourist Shelley Evans, who was found in similar circumstances almost exactly one year ago today. A department press release simply states that there is no sign of foul play or any link between the two tragedies, designating both deaths tragic accidents.

*****

September 22, 1988, 9:57 pm. Route 64, Greenwater Falls County.

"We should have stopped at the last town." Mark sighed. "It was too late to get a motel room anywhere, and we'll never make it to your niece's christening if we stop for the night." He looked across at his wife. "It'll be fine. You're just a bit spooked by what those folks at the truck stop said about this road. It's all just superstitious nonsense, love." He gave her a reassuring smile, catching her hand in his own and giving it a kiss.

Mary smiled. "I guess. It's really creepy out here though."

She glanced back at the road in time to see a young man appear in the path of their headlights. She screamed out a warning and Mark turned just in time to catch a glimpse of the stark fear on the wide-eyed young man's bloodied face before their station wagon collided with his body.

*****

Jake had been trapped in that horrible night on an endless loop, enduring the fear and pain and his own death over and over, until one night everything finally changed.

Instead of his own car running him down, it was a station wagon driven by a young couple. As he watched their panicked search on the road for his body, followed by their relief as they found the corpse of the deer, everything clicked into place.

He understood now how it worked, why that girl had done what she had to him. It wasn't malice, but desperation which had fuelled her actions.

And now, for a chance to escape this hell for once and for all, he would do the same. He felt a brief moment of pity for the couple as he ran them down with their own station wagon, a moment of horror at his own cold actions, before everything finally went blissfully, peacefully dark.

Runner Up
Rob Powell

You can learn more about Rob and his work
at his website:

http://robpowellwrites.com

Daniel Black's Last Book

ROB POWELL

First, let me introduce myself. My name is Daniel Black, or at least that is my pen name, my pseudonym. I am a writer and have been all my life; it is all I'd ever wanted to be from the first time I can remember. Other kids wanted to be astronauts, rocks stars or football players, but for me it has always been the same goal, a writer. Originally I started as a journalist, writing freelance for a number of newspapers and magazines before more recently turning to my lifelong ambition of writing novels.

For the last six months I have been working -- or should I say struggling? -- on my third novel. I have no plot, no character and no idea in where I am going with it. It seems writers block has grabbed me by the bollocks, chewed them up and is enjoying the meal with an immense appetite.

My previous two books had had moderate success but my agent keeps screaming out that they've been lacking something. We need more sales; we need more revenue. As much as I love Jonathon, my agent, I sometimes just want to punch him. However, in all fairness, he may have a point and this time I am determined to write a book that has all the qualities of a best seller.

The main character in my last book was a little flat and lacking depth. Although the reviews were not bad I am not so sure the reader really believed in the character. To be able to create a truly interesting character with some conflict the writer himself must believe. And that was where it fell down, because I rushed the book through for publication.

The first draft for this one is well overdue but I am determined not to sign it off until I am totally satisfied that it is my best work and am comfortable with the whole story. The last two weeks I have been working on the character of Paul; he has been thrown in the bin a few times but there is something about him that draws me back. He's tall, dark and handsome. Or he's fair haired, short and spotty; I just can't get it right. There is also that "something" missing that I've been searching for that has been bugging me. And then, as my mind drifts into daydream mode as I'm on the verge of giving up and am gazing through the window that looks out onto the street, there he stands, staring back through the glass, as real as the day is long. Paul is 6 feet, 3 inches tall, has short brown hair and eyes that pierce through your very soul as they fix their stare on you. The veins on his neck stand out, exaggerated by his muscular physique and he wears a smile that can beguile. Paul's aura exudes control of every situation with effortless charm. Bang! I got it! I can see him and I can feel him; the main character for my next book has arrived.

Fitting Paul into the plot has never been so easy, and as his character grows in strength, the story itself becoming autonomous with the feeling that Paul is writing it himself. Paul effortlessly carves his character with a sinister edge and evil dark force. His charm becomes a weapon to entice unsuspecting souls into his worship sacrifice.

Paul comes from a wealthy background, but had been cut off from his inheritance following a falling-out with his father over a row of jealousy and wealth and never being able to better him. As a result, he'd taken to darker worlds and had committed himself to take all at whatever cost.

"You can have anything you want." Paul sat looking up at the older man with whom he had taken lodgings following the family break up. "Anything you want. But be aware that only Satan can deliver this to you." Paul, angry and wanting all, sat hesitatingly contemplating his options and anticipating having everything. With all his pent up anger, he decides to accept any consequences that at this moment in time seems a small sacrifice.

He met and seduced Jane, his first victim, the neglected wife of a husband that had become so tied up in his work, at her daughter's 18th birthday party. Jane was unable to resist Paul's charms at the party and within an hour of their meeting, she found herself in the bed where she had made love to her husband many times before.

She laid back naked on the sheets, inviting Paul readily. Never had she felt such pleasure than when Paul entered her. The ecstatic feeling had engulfed her whole body, as her fingers clawed chunks of the bedsheets. She screamed out in pleasure as Paul thrust himself inside her.

Opening her eyes, she felt a change in sensation – he was staring down at her with devil-like eyes that displayed no soul, his mouth was rimmed with white foam that was dripping like a savage, rabid dog. a moment later, with that final view of this world impressed on her mind, Paul's mouth opened to reveal sharp yellow and brown fanged teeth. He bit into her throat, pulling at her as a pack of wolves would savage their prey.

Inside, Paul's body was pumping with adrenalin and a feeling of repose. A transformation began to take place. As he walked past the bedroom mirror, Paul's reflection showed a man standing proud and powerful who destined for wealth beyond his wildest dreams. All he had to do was continue to prove his loyalty by finding more souls to sacrifice.

It is amazing to me how easily Paul's character rolled through the story and now, halfway through, it still seemed as if the book was writing itself. I can visualize how Paul sat in the room with me guiding my fingers with the words as I type. I was beginning to believe that this is the book I was waiting for. This is the one that will put my name in the hall of fame along with other great writers of my time. Paul's eyes locked on the two girls in the centre of the dance floor. Oblivious to the beat of the music as it vibrated the room, his stare remained fixed and unshaken. The girls, in their early twenties, left the floor and headed towards the bar together

– both had simultaneously felt the presence of eyes upon them. Before they realized who or where this feeling had been coming from they were accepting drinks from Paul. Linda took her glass and smiled back at Paul with a seductive look. This is going to be an easy conquest, Paul thought to himself, considering the alcohol-infused mirth of the girls whilst his mind's eye visually constructed his plan.

After taking the bottle of chilled white wine from his fridge, he opened it and poured three glasses. He took only a moment to feel the coldness of the liquid through the glasses on his fingers before he handed one each to Lucy and Linda. Absorbing every moment as if it was in slow motion, he sat in the armchair opposite the young ladies and observed the drunkenness of his intended prey, giving them a charming smile.

The girls giggled back at him, looked at each other then, and Lucy reached up to run her hands through Linda's hair. She pulled her friend's face towards hers, opened her mouth and slid her tongue inside Linda's mouth. Paul took a slow and thoughtful drink of wine, thoroughly enjoying the show. After a while, he placed his glass on the table next to the armchair, stood up and moved towards the girls.

The dawn light shone through onto the bed where Paul laid in the middle of Lucy's and Linda's naked bodies. The bed was sodden with blood, and Paul's mouth was still red and wet. Paul stood up and moved to the end of the bed. He looked down at his victims and smiled contentedly, but a sudden sharp pain in his stomach makes him realize that his work had still not been completed. He took another look at the mangled bodies of the girls – they'd been young, yes, but not pure. To get total power, to get everything that he wants, it is necessary that he take a virgin as a sacrifice for Satan.

As he pondered this challenge, he remembered Jane's daughter who had recently celebrated her 18th birthday. That night, Jane had spoken of her daughter and how her innocence would have been shattered if she'd found her mother and Paul together. He felt sure that she would be the perfect victim to help him fulfill his commitment. Paul gently knocked at the door and within a minute Isabelle opened the it. Her face was grey, her eyes sad, and her sweet mouth drawn into a frown. As he looked deep into her eyes, he felt convinced that she would be the perfect sacrifice.

"I came to pay my condolences," he said softly to her. "I knew your mother only briefly. She was a very kind woman."

Isabelle invited Paul into her living room. She sat down on the sofa, thanked Paul for coming by and offered him a drink.

"Thank you, but let me get it," Paul answered. He rose from the leather armchair and walked over to the drink cabinet behind the sofa where Isabelle sat and poured himself a whisky.

"Fine drink your father has." He walked over to the desk in the corner of the room and picked up a shiny letter opener. Before Isabelle can look around, Paul plunged it with such force into the back of her head that it protruded through the front of her forehead. Paul extracted the weapon carefully, then walked back to the desk and calmly placed the letter opener back in its proper place.

I look down and see the blood still wet on the letter opener, blotting the pages of my third novel. And there, on the sofa in my office, lays my daughter Christine, motionless, her eyes sorrowful and hauntingly dead, with her stare fixed on me ….

Runner Up

Stephen Kriedemann

Me... and My Shadow

STEPHEN KRIEDEMANN

"Me and my shadow… Strolling down the avenue… Me and my shadow… Not a soul to tell our troubles to…" - Me and My Shadow (Billy Rose, 1927)

We all have that one friend. You know the one I mean, the negative influence… the friend with the bad ideas who gets you into troubled situations. These are the people most of us grow apart from over time as we age.

But I can't get free of mine. For better or for worse, I'm stuck with him. You see, for me, that troublesome friend is my Shadow… and he's an asshole and a bloody psychopath!

It all began back when I was just a child. I was a quiet kid who always had a hard time making friends. I spent a lot of time by myself reading, and with a great imagination, I cured my loneliness as a tot by creating myself some imaginary friends.

Shadow didn't like them. One by one, all of my imaginary friends met an untimely end thanks to Shadow.

First to go were Dot and Dash, my brother and sister duo of imaginary friends. I was an only child, raised by a single mother in a small rural community. I longed for a family unit that I just didn't have, so I made up my own siblings to help me through my childhood.

I had a summer of great adventures with Dot and Dash when I was about seven years old. We spent our days out in the sun, exploring the woods on our property, fishing in the pond and building a tree fort in the old oak behind our house.

This is where Dash became Shadow's first victim. While building our tree fort, Shadow pushed Dash from the top of the ladder. Dash fell 20 feet, landing broken and bloodied on the wood pile below.

I was traumatized, and Dot was heartbroken. Shadow just leaned his head back and laughed silently. He never explained his actions, but I knew he was just jealous of Dash.

I ran, sobbing to my mother to tell her what had happened.

"Shadow did it mom!" I exclaimed, but she just told me to stop being foolish and run along to play.

Poor Dot was next, a few months later that summer. She was still very upset about losing Dash, and she didn't trust Shadow at all, which just seemed to amuse him. He reveled in her fear and disdain for him.

As we sat at the pond fishing one afternoon, Dot was complaining again about Shadow's presence, asking why I was still friends with him after what he had done.

Having heard enough, Shadow bashed Dot across the back of the head with a log and pushed her into the pond.

I ran along the water's edge, screaming and yelling for help. I was just a kid, and I couldn't swim, so I watched helplessly as another friend died at the hands of Shadow, as her lifeless body slowly sank beneath the water's surface.

My mother came running over in response to the commotion, and was furious with my explanation for the panic.

"He did it, Mom! Shadow hit her and pushed her in and now she's dead, Mom!"

My mother just told me to stop being childish and wasting her time. She couldn't see the body and didn't believe what I had seen. That night she read me 'The Boy Who Cried Wolf'. I remember thinking to myself, that wolf has nothing on Shadow!

This behaviour continued for years, through my childhood and into my teens. I lost a couple more imaginary friends before I resigned myself to living as a loner. Shadow still seemed determined to make my life miserable, destroying anything that I valued.

Teddy, the stuffed bear my grandparents had given to me when I was born, was eviscerated on the dining room table one afternoon. The framed photo I had of my father was repeatedly smashed when thrown across the room. Twice my bookcase, containing all of the books that allowed my mind to wander to better places, were ravaged. They were set on fire and thrown around the room. The second time the fire spread and almost took the house with it!

And every time Shadow acted like an asshole, the same thing happened. I told my mother, and she never believed me. I was getting too old for this, and needed to take responsibility for my own actions.

It got even worse in my teenage years, and high school was a terrible experience. Shadow always found new ways to screw with me. My mate's teacher caught Shadow gesticulating sexually towards her in class, which earned me my first suspension. The football team took issue when Shadow gave the quarterback the finger in the cafeteria.

They never believed me when I said it wasn't me, that I had done nothing and Shadow was setting me up. I was weird and antisocial; nobody ever gave a second thought to my story and my plight.

The final straw came when the school secretary saw a projection on the principal's glass door of Shadow making a throat slitting motion as I was getting in trouble for one of his other pranks. This 'threat' officially got me kicked out of school, and sent home to be alone with my mother and Shadow.

Shunned by the kids in town, the rest of my teen years were spent trapped on our property, just me, Shadow and my mom, who still did not believe my stories of Shadow. She tried to alleviate my boredom by enrolling me in correspondence classes to finish my high school diploma. This worked out well, actually.

She also thought she could help with my loneliness by getting me a pet to play with, but that didn't work out quite as well. The first few pets were almost explainable, the fish jumped out of their tank, even though they were methodically laid out side by side, on the shelf above the tank. The bird must have been ripped apart by the cat, and the cat must have crawled into the chimney earlier, before we lit the fireplace…

At some point a pattern became clear to my mom, and the pets stopped. We snared a few small animals in traps after, but that wasn't enjoyable for Shadow who didn't want to find them dead, he wanted to kill them.

I buried each of them, or what was left of them, by the pond not far from where Dot had been dealt her death blow many years before. Every time Shadow watched silently as I cleaned up his deeds. What could he really say, I guess?

As I grew into a young man in my 20s, my life became even more of a challenge with Shadow around. No matter what job I got, Shadow found a way to get me fired. Whether offending clients, coworkers or bosses, or being destructive, it often cost me more in damages than I ever made during the short time I worked there.

It was following one such occurrence, after the police had dropped me at home with another mischief charge, that Shadow went from being an asshole to being a complete psychopath!

Shadow thought it would be funny to ruin my new job stocking shelves at the grocery store by inserting sewing needles into baby products. This stupid prank earned me my new mischief charge, and a hefty $6,500 bill for damages to replace stock, which we couldn't afford to pay.

I heard the police officer telling my mom I was a local menace who needed help, and that I should be put away. Everyone thought I was crazy, always acting out and blaming this mysterious Shadow. Nobody had ever believed me about him. If anything was driving me crazy, it was this disbelief that I continued to encounter. No matter what Shadow did, or how often, he seemed destined to always get away with it, leaving me holding the bag.

When the police drove away, my mother went into a tirade. She'd been dealing with over twenty years of this shit, and she couldn't take it anymore. Her son was an overgrown child with mental problems. We were going to lose the house paying for this crazy behaviour and she wished that I had never been born.

That's when it happened.

To this day I don't know if Shadow was just sick of listening to her, or if in some twisted way he was trying to help and defend me, but he snapped into a murderous rage. I watched as he beat my mother mercilessly, tossing her around the room like a rag doll, breaking furniture and shattering bones in my mother's all-too-frail body.

But then I couldn't watch any more. In horror I turned my head away, and, instead focused my gaze on the flickering images on the wall cast by the chandelier rocking back and forth above, of Shadow choking the life out of my mother. I could see the shadow of her arms flailing, and her hands grasping at Shadow's as she desperately tried to breathe again.

She didn't – and never would. I lay on the floor sobbing for hours, looking at my mother's limp body and considering what would be done to me once she was discovered, since there was no way anyone would believe that Shadow had done such a despicable deed. They'd never believed before; they wouldn't start now.

So the next morning at dawn, Shadow and I silently buried my mother in the now-familiar grounds by the pond. I would later mark the spot with a bench built of wood salvaged from the old tree fort that had taken Dash from me. This spot had become a makeshift burial ground and memorial spot.

And again Shadow said nothing while we buried his latest conquest.

This time however, the silence spoke volumes. This time, the rules of the game had changed. From now on, it would be just us, Shadow and I, alone together.

If only I had known then that the next twenty years would see so many bodies added to this burial ground, perhaps I would have gone to the police and told them my story. Perhaps I should have… My life may not have been that much better or worse; however, it would have made a world of difference for all of the others.

Like Christy, the blonde teller at the bank who, after flirting with me once a week for a few years, finally gave up waiting for me to act normal and told me I would be escorting her to the county fair back in my 2twenty eighth year.

She was a beautiful, sweet soul, and the first girl who had ever really shown any interest in me, probably because she only saw me within the confines of the bank. She didn't know me well enough to know my odd reputation, or to have heard of my hassles with Shadow.

But she had her own hassles with Shadow in the end. We dated a few times before we ended up back at the house for a few drinks. Here I was thinking this would be the night I lost my over-ripened virginity. I should have known things would go horribly wrong.

Once it was clear that Christy wasn't as eager as I was to move our relationship to the next level, Shadow became agitated and I knew the horrors that would follow. I turned away from Christy as he bashed in her face with his heavy, pounding fists. All I saw were the shadows and blood splashing the walls.

Or there was that pimple faced paper boy, I never did catch his name. Stupid kid couldn't toss a paper to save his life and always missed the mark. Shadow didn't miss the mark when he set a trip wire between the trees on the path he whizzed along to get to our house. Damn near took the kids head right off.

There was old Doc Tom, nice enough to see me after hours. He had been my doctor for years and was worried about me. I was in my thirties and should have some friends, or maybe a lady friend. I guess Shadow took umbrage about being ignored or not considered by the doc, whose old neck snapped like a twig under Shadow's heavy hand.

I think Betty happened in my thirties as well. She was the first hitchhiker I picked up, just passing through the area on her way to nowhere. Well, she made a few too many cracks about us rural folk and Shadow cut her up in the road, as I watched the terrible scene projected in the high beams across the concrete.

By the time I was facing my fourtieth birthday I had to admit that this would forever be my lot in life, alone except for my Shadow, and always left to clean up his messes. I had already lost so much and buried so many. I gave up fighting the evil inside Shadow and tried my best to just minimize contact with the general public.

Which has worked pretty well for the last couple of decades now. Oh sure, there's been a dozen or so transients, hitchhikers, salesmen and the such come by over the years, but we're pretty secluded out here. I've often wondered how different my story might have been if I'd been born and raised in a large urban centre like Vancouver or Toronto?

Anyways, so that's how we come to where we are today, with you here tied up in the back seat listening to my twisted tale of a frightening friendship. I know it will be of little comfort to you during the last few days of your life, but I thought you deserved some explanation. I will of course be there with you throughout your ordeal, although I can do nothing to stop him, since I have conceded to the fact that he does not heed my cries of disgust or my begging for mercy.

I still can't watch him do the things he does, but I will be there by his side, head turned away, watching the Shadow on the wall.

"Just me and my shadow… All alone and feelin' blue…"

Second Place Winner

E. J. Walker

Facebook Author Page: facebook.com/ejwalkerwrites/

ejwalkerwrites.wordpress.com

Trail's End

E.J. Walker

Birdsong dripped through the awakening forest in liquid-sounding squeaks and squelches. Thomas rubbed the greasy stubble on his chin and squinted at the form lying beside him in the small tent. Suzanne was on her back, snoring. Time to move, he thought, but he didn't. He could just stay in bed. His wife would rise and start breakfast. He would sit up, wrapped in the warmth of the sleeping bag, and drink black coffee while they planned the day. This had been their routine for the last three days: wake up, breakfast, hike, and then make camp. Routine was about to change.

The morning air was damp, and it made the sleeping bag cling to his legs when he tried to kick free. Condensation coated the inside of the tent fly and streamed down the mesh walls wherever the two fabrics met. He reached behind his head for the roll of plastic wrap, and his bare arm brushed a wet spot. The chill sent an involuntary shiver through his torso and into his toes.

In the half-light, Suzanne was almost pretty. He reached for her and slipped one hand beneath her head. His fingers combed the oily softness of her dark hair. She smiled and murmured something, her eyes still closed.

Thomas locked that peaceful expression onto her face with the first layer of freezer wrap. She startled awake before he got the roll around her head a second time. Pinning her with all his weight, he fought the violent bucking as she struggled, arms trapped inside the mummy-style bag and fighting for breath he wouldn't give her. He pressed his own sleeping bag into her face and bore down harder. The strangled, mewling sound became less audible as the heaving softened into shudders. Thomas imagined body surfing a wave and staying on top of it until he skidded to a stop in a roil of foam and sand.

Finally, the shaking stopped altogether, and he lay there listening to his own breathing return to normal. Birds, and the gurgle of a nearby stream, were the only other sounds. Suzanne was silent. He uncovered her to check, and saw the she looked surprisingly serene under her clear, suffocating mask. Her eyes were closed and a hint of a smile played across her barely-parted lips. Aside from a thin film of mucous trapped around her nose and mouth, not a hint of the violent struggle a few minutes earlier was evident. She looked as though she were asleep. He zipped her up inside of the sleeping bag so that he didn't have to look at her face, and hurriedly dressed. There was much to do.

An hour later he was at the hole, unwrapping the tools he'd stored there months before. Thomas was a leader in a local outdoor club, and he was in charge of maintaining this section of trail. Carrying tools around in the backcountry was expected of him. He was very familiar with the area and spent most weekends doing maintenance work: cutting back overgrowth, clearing drainages, and identifying areas that needed the more extensive attention of a trail crew. He also used that time, and the tools, to dig the five-foot-deep hole in front of him now.

He'd selected the spot almost a year ago, not long after he'd begun seeing Melissa intimately. Suzanne and Melissa had been friends since college, staying close through rounds of children, and, in Melissa's case, husbands, until middle age had overtaken, then passed them. Needing something to fill their lives, they'd opened a small art gallery on a whim. It had been wildly successful—way beyond anyone's hopes. The enterprise had been so lucrative, in fact, that Thomas had been able to retire early, and he now helped out around the shop when needed. He was closing the store one evening with Melissa when Suzanne was out of town. That night his relationship with both women, along with everything else in his life, had forever changed. Somehow, he'd kept the affair secret. Melissa was like a drug that he couldn't resist—and she had plans.

Thomas set the mattock and shovel down beside the hole and dumped in the contents of Suzanne's backpack. An unexpected sadness fell over him when he saw her belongings scattered below in the dirt. The laughably-bright-green, waterproof wallet was a Christmas gift he'd bought years back. Inside, he knew were photos of kids, grandkids, and the faded wedding picture of them standing in front of a gaudy, daisy-themed cake. Folding up the plastic sheet, he stuffed that into the pack, along with the pruning saw.

He wanted to call Melissa, to let her know that things were on track, but didn't dare. There wouldn't be phone reception, anyway. Melissa would have to wait. That was her part of the act. She was at a parking area "waiting" for Suzanne to hike out alone on a side trail. By nightfall, when she hadn't shown up, Melissa was supposed to call police about an overdue hiker. Thomas would continue up the main trail, supposedly oblivious that his wife was missing, for another two days, or until someone caught up to inform him. There would be a massive search that would turn up nothing. He expected some scrutiny, sure, but Suzanne was an experienced hiker, and they did this very same, two-part trip once or twice a year. He could play the grief-wrought-husband-desperately-searching-for-missing-wife role well enough to make it work.

He almost missed the small path branching off the trail to the campsite—and he was looking for it. Smiling, he turned and threaded his way over the jumble of rocks and red spruce, careful not to disturb the carpet of moss that covered everything. He would have to make several more trips back to the hole and he didn't want someone wandering into the campsite by accident. Fifty yards later the tent popped into view. He froze mid-step. The door was open.

Never taking his eyes from the door, Thomas skirted the tree line in a wide arc around the tent. The tent fly dangled motionless, half covering the opening. The mesh body was open as well. He'd made sure both were zipped tight before he'd left. Pretty sure. Leaving it open would have been inexcusably careless, but he had been rushing. He nearly fell, and then made too much noise scrambling to keep his feet. He took a breath and forced himself relax.

"It's not like I'm going to wake anyone up." He said it aloud, and laughed as he did, but the stark sound of the words did little to boost his confidence. An odd jerkiness in his legs made the distance to the tent seem farther away than it was. Once there, he reached for the nylon flap and pulled it aside. A cold whirlpool drained from his chest to his belly. Suzanne's sky-blue colored sleeping bag lay stretched out along the length of the tent. It was unzipped and empty. He focused on the darker circle midway up the goose down-filled fabric. In the end, she'd wet it.

Hairs on the back of his neck tingled while he slowly turned around. The campsite was empty. A line dangled, slack from a tree branch near the clearing's edge. His backpack should have been on one end, safely hauled up and away from animals' reaches. Now that was gone, too, along with his phone, map, compass, food water filter and everything else he needed to exist in the backcountry.

Granted, it had taken longer, been messier and more brutal than he thought, but he'd finished the job, hadn't he? He'd checked for a pulse, right? Smacking his forehead with the heel of his palm, he fought down a wave of rising panic. He hadn't listened for a heartbeat! He'd botched the one thing he'd ABSOLUTELY needed to get right. Somehow, he'd left her alive, and she'd taken off with his pack.

"Fuck. Fuck. Fuck me Jesus, Mary and Joseph…fuck!" He repeated the chant over and over while he raced up the trail, in the direction he figured she must have gone.

After fifteen minutes with no sign of her, he stopped and almost turned around. Then he saw it. A few feet off the trail and down the hill, a sock hung off a waist-high vine. It was one of his spare pair of Darn Tough socks. A moment later, he noticed the game trail and followed it into a seemingly impassible jumble of rocks and snags. The path disappeared at times, and then he would pick it up again just when he was ready to abandon the side trip.

He clambered over a huge fallen log thick with brown moss and paused to catch his breath. On the other side, on the path, lay a page torn from a book. It was from Stephen King's Cell, the book he'd been carrying in his backpack. Thomas took a breath and pondered just what he would do once he caught up to his wife. Beg forgiveness? A bit late for that, he supposed. No, he decided, setting down the near-empty pack and taking out the saw, there was but one ending to this story. And it wasn't going to be a neat one.

A trail of book pages led him deeper into a marl of deadfalls and moss-slickened rocks where the temperature fell and direct sunlight seemed to seldom touch. The trail stopped at the edge of a large cirque, and he stared down into a boulder-field at the bottom of a hundred-foot, sheer drop. It was insane-looking terrain that seemed to stretch on forever.

A twig-snap and flutter of movement at his vision's edge made him whirl, but not quickly enough. Something solid hit him, and over the edge he tumbled. Flashes of green, blue and gray flew past in a blur, and then it went all black.

"You'll be wanting to keep this, won't you? Pictures of the kids and all." The voice was familiar. A woman's. But he couldn't seem to keep thoughts together long enough bring up an image of the person speaking. I should know this one, he thought, then started to fade out again. Searing pain shot across his shoulders and through his upper back. Someone was dragging him over rocks. Maybe by the feet. Nothing registered below his shoulders.

"Yeah, toss me that, please. All my I.D. is in there as well. Everything else gets buried."

It was another woman. Something green arced across his line of sight then disappeared. He couldn't turn his head to track it.

"Ma…?" his own voice surprised him.

"Ah, look who's awake," the closest one cooed. Warm breath tickled his ear. A face hovered a foot above his. It was upside-down Suzanne, wearing a shimmering Saran Wrap scarf. "Hello, darling." Her voice was breathily sensuous. "Kind of a harsh wake-up call this morning, don't you think?"

"Help. Back. Broken." He barely got the words out. They were whispers on little puffs of air that seem to die on his lips.

"Yeah, I'd say you're right there, but I wouldn't worry much about that, right now, honey." She laughed and he suddenly didn't like where she placed spoken emphasis in the sentence.

"Oh my God," screamed the other woman. Suzanne grabbed his hair and tilted his head so that he could see. He gasped with the pain. Things in his neck crunched. Melissa emerged from the hole he'd dug. She pointed to his waist. "He's got a fucking boner!"

Suzanne's mouth curled into a half-smile, and her eyes widened. "You do!" She clapped her hands. "I've read about this. Sometimes men with spinal injuries get erections. It's some kind of autonomic reflex." She pulled at his clothes. "Thar she blows!"

They both laughed, and Thomas felt the world spin.

"You might get one more ride outta that pony," Melissa said. "Want me to go for a walk?"

"No." Suzanne pulled Melissa close and kissed her mouth. Both women turned to him and grinned. Their eyes glowed amber and their mouths filled with rows of tiny, jagged teeth. "You're not the only one with a little secret," Suzanne said, and patted his forehead. "Here's your chance to stay in that cozy little place you dug out of the ground just for me." She lifted her chin at the hole, and a gray tentacle uncoiled and rolled out from her mouth.

"Sit back, babe." Melissa held up a saw. "And leave the driving to us."

Third Place Winner

Guy Cheston

Guy lives with his wife and son in Virginia. A writer with a day job, he pursues the craft at night after his family has settled in. When he's not reading or writing, he likes to jog. He has an eleven year old black cat that he's convinced is possessed, or insane, or something like that You can find Guy online :

Twitter: @guycheston

www.guycheston.com

Blood of a Sinner

GUY CHESTON

Father Vince jabbered on in Latin while Jimmy fiddled with his iPod in the back pew. He was smushed between an odorific old fart and Linda, his foster mother. The smelly old guy was sleeping and Linda seemed enraptured in the priest's babbling Latin. As long as she stayed that way, he could keep playing his game. He didn't want to be at St. Vincent's church for a Hallowe'en Eve service. It was an old, stupid tradition that nobody else did anymore…except for here.

Heck if he knew why.

A thwap across the back of Jimmy's head made him jump and he looked up to see Linda staring at him with a menacing gaze that teetered on the brink of hatred.

"Not in church," she said, and yanked the iPod away and stuffed it into her pocket, then thwapped him on the head again.

So much for her not finding out. Mean ole bitch.

He knew that ten-year-old's weren't supposed to cuss, but a mean ole bitch was a mean ole bitch. There just wasn't any better way to describe his heavyset middle-aged wannabe mother. He would report her for hitting him if he didn't have such a bad reputation with child services as a chronic liar. Adults never listened to kids, anyway. Unless he was bruised and broken, they'd ignore him.

He crammed his hands in the pockets of his too-small sweater and leaned forward, staring at his over-sized shoes. The next hour was an agonizing repetition of praying, kneeling, singing, and listening to Latin as the priest droned on and on.

Afterward, when they pulled out of the parking lot and came to a red light at an intersection a block away from the church, Linda unleashed another one of her lectures. Her breath was ripe, a mixture of cigarettes and coffee, teeth a stained yellow that could have belonged to a corpse.

"Jimmy, your parents' death was a horrible accident, and I know you've been bounced around in a handful of different homes since you were a toddler. But the one thing you need to remember about me is how seriously I take church. And why, because"

"There's evil in the world that we can't see."

"Don't interrupt me, or so help me I'll pop you another before we get home. But that's right. There's evil we can see, like all that death going on in the Middle East, and there's evil we can't see. The only way to survive against the unseen is by learning to harden yourself to it."

"Is that why you hit me?"

Even in the dark car Jimmy could tell Linda was rolling her eyes.

"You talk like I beat you, Jimmy. But a couple of good wallops on the head teaches more to a boy than a hundred hours in a time out chair."

"You gave me a bloody nose last week."

Linda smacked a hand against the steering wheel. "Modern day parenting has made our children weak. You need to be strong; and you know why. What's my favorite verse?"

"First Peter five eight. The Devil walks about like a roaring lion, seeking whom he may devour."

"That's right. And strong parents breed strong children. You came to me weak, which means that your parents were weak, but as the good Lord is my witness I swear I'll make you strong."

He dug his fingers into the cushion of the seat so hard he thought his nails might snap off. He gritted his teeth so a sarcastic reply wouldn't spew out of him and get him hit again. But the anger bloomed in his chest, red hot, and he couldn't hold it in anymore. She'd hit him too many times; and if social services wouldn't help then he'd have to try somewhere else.

"I hate you."

The blow to his face sent the side of his head smacking into the window.

"Children, obey your parents in the Lord, for this is right."

Jimmy unbuckled the seat-belt and opened the car door, then spat at his tormentor. He suppressed a grin as Linda reeled back in the dark and wiped the loogie from her chin.

"Provoke not your children to wrath, bitch," he said, and slammed the door as hard as he could, then took off running. He was pretty sure that verse about not provoking children was in the Bible somewhere, but it definitely didn't end with the B word.

Stupefied by panic and catapulted by adrenaline, he darted into the woods, heading in the direction of the church and hoping the priest would help.

Linda yelled something from far behind. He heard a car door open as he raised his hands to shield himself from thick foliage. A flashlight beam illuminated the path ahead. He charged forward, zig-zagging in between trees and hoping to lose her.

Linda might have a flashlight, but her weight and age made her slow. After a couple of minutes, the flashlight became a speck in the woods behind him. The last thing he needed to do right now was to face plant into a tree and knock himself out. At this point, if she found him and dragged him back to the car, the beating he would get might finish him for good.

If he went in a straight line, eventually the woods would spit him back out close to the church. He kept hoping Linda would give up and go back to her car and call the cops. That would give him more time to get to St.

Vincent's. But she didn't. Linda was slow, but persistent. Ox-like. The only way to beat her was to stay out of reach.

Another several minutes of dodging through the brush brought him to the outer perimeter of St. Vincent's cemetery. The exterior of the huge cathedral spiked into the cold October night, the cross at the top flush with the full moon. The cemetery was protected by a black iron fence several feet high that loomed over the dead, sinister and grim.

He stayed in the tree line and followed the fence around until he came to the graveyard's entrance. The fastest way into the church was through the back door, so he shot out of the woods and sprinted passed the gate and hid behind a huge tombstone.

The flashlight beam erupted from the trees. He raced to another tombstone and crouched as Linda entered the graveyard. She was searching the other side of the cemetery when Jimmy heard another set of footsteps going in Linda's direction.

"Father Vince, thank the Lord," Linda said. Jimmy's heart fell. His abuser had tormented him relentlessly for a year, and now she'd beaten him to the man he'd hoped to confess her crimes to.

"My child, what brings you here to the resting place of the dead, on a night like this?"

"It's Jimmy. He ran from the car. I think he came this way. Have you seen him?"

"I'm afraid not, my dear. But the Lord will provide. I was out here praying to Him, and my prayers have been answered. He has provided to us on this holy night; for He has brought us you."

Then came a wet thunk. Jimmy peered out from his hiding spot and saw Linda's flashlight beam shining in an arc on the ground, unmoving. The shadowy shape of Father Vince lurched backwards, grunting. Jimmy followed. As he drew nearer, things became more clear.

Father Vince dragged Jimmy's unconscious foster mother into the church.

*****

It took summoning all the courage he could to walk through the door. He hated Linda, couldn't give a crap what the priest did to her. Yet, burning curiosity drove him to follow. Inside, he walked down a dim hallway until it came to an intersection.

He noticed a spatter of fresh blood leading to the right. He followed the trail and came to a door. Jimmy pressed an ear to it and heard voices. They were muttering something in a low, rhythmic way. It wasn't singing, no. More like chanting.

Hands shaking, a single bead of sweat sliding down the center of his forehead to the crest of his nose, Jimmy turned the knob and stepped inside. He'd entered the auditorium through a side door. He crouched behind a pew to hide from the people gathered in the front.

Candles lining the auditorium walls provided the only lighting and made the group of black-robed worshipers resemble an assembly of shadows. They encircled a stone table, upon which Linda rested. She groaned as she came to, struggling, her outstretched limbs strapped down. Father Vince stood above the procession behind his podium, leading the chorus of chanters.

The cadence rose in pitch for a few seconds, then stopped as Linda screamed. The noise wracked Jimmy's skull and made him crouch even lower. He wanted to be brave, to maybe do something; but terror anchored him in place. Paralyzed with fear and hidden by the dark, all he could do was watch.

"Silence her," said Father Vince, who ran his hands down his robe, smoothing its creases.

One of Linda's captors stuffed a rag in her mouth.

"We almost didn't have an offering for this night. I searched and searched, but then my prayers to the dead were answered. She appeared almost out of nowhere, searching for a lost child. The Lord will provide."

"The Lord will provide," the assembly repeated.

Jimmy was beginning to wonder what lord they were talking about. His nose caught a whiff of something earthy and he turned his head to see another black-robed worshiper carrying a goat down the center aisle toward the procession. It mewed pitifully. The group parted to allow the man through. He held the goat atop Linda and withdrew a dagger, then sliced the animal's neck. A gout of blood sprayed his foster mother. The man rested the dying goat on Linda's stomach.

Father Vince thumped a giant book onto the podium.

It didn't look anything like any Bible he'd ever seen. It started doing something he'd never seen a Bible do.

As the priest resumed his chanting, the tome opened by itself and began to levitate. It slowly slid out from the podium until it was hovering above Linda, throbbing with malignance. A thick black mist spewed from the book and fell to the table, where it blotted out Linda's body. A voice came from the book, deep and archaic, neither male nor female.

"I smell the blood of a sinner. An abuser of children. A hypocrite."

Father Vince moved from behind his podium, then knelt and bowed his head as he spoke.

"Oh, Lord. We offer you this sacrifice on the eve of your holy night."

"I accept your offering. But I also smell the blood of the sinless."

A talon-like hand clamped down on the back of Jimmy's shirt and jerked him up. He hadn't been paying attention to what was behind him. There must have been someone there the whole time.

"Let me go!"

As he drew nearer, a yearning moan sounded from the tome. The mist morphed as it solidified over Linda. A face formed; and even through the candle-lit blackness, Jimmy could tell the being was unimaginably handsome and beautiful. Despite Jimmy's terror, a longing stirred within him to reach out and brush his hand against the pristine face.

"Forbidden fruit is the sweetest," said the being. Its mouth opened wide as a black, skeletal arm came through it and formed into a hand when it reached Jimmy's head, trailing in front of a swirling string of darkness. And as though reading his thoughts, it did to him what he'd wanted to do to it. Fingers brushed his face. They were warm and a little wet, muddy. They started at the top of his forehead and slid downward. It was a soothing feeling and made him sleepy. The fingers traced along his lips, squeezing them together playfully. Then a finger slid into his mouth and made him gag. It tasted of rot, thick with death. He tried to jerk his head away but the power of the being within the mist held him in place. The finger danced around in his mouth, swirling, sliding its wet, fetid nastiness along his tongue.

Abruptly, it yanked its finger out of his mouth and retreated into the black cloud, the human form vanishing as a howl echoed from the book.

"He who dwells above will not let me have this one. Innocent now, but not for long. Until then, let him forget."

Denied the tender offering of a child, the being took its violence out on Linda. Her cries turned to shrieks as the mist opened to show disfigured claws scraping at her body. The claws turned to fists and pummeled her with pitiless savagery, pounding her face so hard that blood spouted out the back of her head as it cracked against the altar, streams of red trickling down the edges and puddling into massive bowls that waited on the floor. The fists opened and long nails sliced open her chest cavity. His foster mother jerked and writhed on the altar as a dark hand plunged into the folds of skin beneath her left breast in a spray of red, wrenching out her beating heart and squashing it in a cry of rage. The mist closed and blew toward Jimmy as he fought against an unstoppable desire to sleep.

*****

Father Vince woke him at sunrise. Jimmy sat up in an empty church. He was exhausted, and the pressure of trying to find his foster mother had drained him of energy. On the way home from the Hallows Eve service, she'd come to an intersection down the road and snapped, swerving the car to the side of the road and running away. He'd tried to follow her down the path he thought she'd ran and found that it led back to the church. Unable to find her, Jimmy had decided to settle into the front pew and sleep. Father Vince would be here in the morning.

The altar below the podium shined bright and gave off a pine scent, as though it had just been polished. Jimmy explained Linda's breakdown to the Father and they'd searched the church for Linda. Everyone always knew she had issues, and most people thought it was a miracle that social services had cleared her to be a foster parent. They couldn't find her. After the priest phoned social services, Jimmy ate a breakfast of jellied toast and orange juice in the nice man's office, which for some reason smelled metallic and coppery. A little bit like blood.

"We will find her, Jimmy, but I think you'll probably be changing homes again. Can't have someone irresponsible caring for your well-being, can we. Until then, I will try to arrange for you to stay with the church's boarding school. Do you have any idea what you want to dress up as tonight for the Hallowe'en party?"

Jimmy shrugged. He didn't like Linda anyway; so he didn't care whether they found her or not. What he did care about was what he was going to be tonight. A strange aching stirred within him to be clad in black. He couldn't get an image out of his head of a hooded, black-robed monk holding a gigantic, ancient book. He told the priest about the costume idea.

Father Vince nodded and smiled, then said, "I'll see what I can do."

A Horror Anthology

48

Fourth Place Winner (Tie)

Caito Caol

My Friend Bruce

CAITO CAOL

"Robert, you've been very quiet today." The woman sitting across from me pushed that repulsive smattering of frizz she called 'bangs' off her high forehead and brought her hand back down onto the notebook that she held on her lap. It always remained open, but she never wrote in it. Pissed me off.

"Robert, perhaps you might want to start talking about your friend that you mentioned in our last session… Bruce was it?"

She fucking knew it was Bruce. Probably wrote that down last week, after I left, with her tiny, prematurely arthritic fingers onto the goddamned blank pages of her shitty little notebook. *Robert.* Was I in trouble or something? Only my mother called me Robert, and frankly that bitch can burn in hell. I suppose I was in some trouble. The woman at work that complained about my quote, unquote "behaviour" seemed to really enjoy all that trouble until she squeaked to management and landed me in a month-long "voluntary" counseling nightmare.

"Robert?" Fuck woman, shut your face before I shut it for you.

"Yes, sorry, what? I was thinking."

"I thought you could tell me a bit about your friend, Bruce."

"What do you want to know?"

"Why don't you start from the beginning?"

Bruce was a fucked up kid. I had probably seen him around, but the first time I really noticed him was the day the teacher threw his slate across the classroom when he wouldn't stop writing with his left hand. She'd laid his hand across her desk and took the ruler to it until it was so battered that he had no choice but to write sloppily with his right hand. He hadn't made a noise through the whole thing. He'd locked eyes with me across the room and stared at me with no fear, no desperation, as the ruler landed again and again on his thin, pale fingers. I obviously wanted to look away, like all the other kids did. I wanted to whimper when a fingernail detached with a small spurt of blood onto the faded, moldy blue shirt Bruce wore every single day of his life. Sure, I wanted to jump up and yell at the teacher to stop, but instead I sat there, gritting my teeth so hard I was certain they would explode through my cheeks like tiny porcelain shrapnel. And I held his stare. I am not sure why he stared at me the way he did; maybe he just needed to lock eyes with anyone to help distract him from the pain? But for what felt like an eternity, I existed in a bubble with nothing except Bruce and the pain that I hoped he couldn't feel.

A few days later, I spotted a crusty cotton bandage on the hand of a boy walking on the dirt road that juts out from the main road I walked on to get home. I knew my mother would wallop my ass if I was late for supper, but I turned on the dirt road and followed Bruce at a brisk walk. I didn't think I would catch up to him so quickly, but he was certainly in no rush to get home. I caught up to him before I could come up with a reason for why I was following him in the first place.

Bruce spun around with more startled fear than would seem appropriate for a boy hearing footfalls behind him in the broad daylight, but he relaxed when he saw me. It was almost as if he knew I was coming at some point. I started to make up a story about how I knew someone who lived on the road and I needed to drop off a book, but when I looked around I realized that there were no other houses on this road. Bruce looked at me in the way you look at someone pityingly when they are caught in a lie and I immediately dropped the bullshit. I walked next to him at his achingly slow pace in silence for a while.

Finally, he looked up at me, told me that I really should go home before my mother kicked my ass, and then carried on without another word, leaving me standing alone in the eddies of swirling dust. I watched him turn onto a long laneway, visibly steeling himself to approach the dilapidated farmhouse with white paint bubbling off the wood like a blistering sun burn. I didn't hesitate another moment, turning on my heel and running home as fast as I could. My mother beat me within an inch of my life.

The next day, Bruce chose to forgo his usual seat in the back of the classroom and came to sit next to me. I would find myself staring at him painstakingly printing every letter on his slate with as much care as could be rendered with his right hand. The effect was sloppy at best, but he was so determined. Over the weeks that followed, Bruce made a permanent resident of the desk next to mine and every once in a while, with decreasing rarity, he would look at me. He had a beautiful smile. His front teeth were turned in and grey but when he smiled I could see the exuberant boy that hid beneath his frail, stoic exterior. He would sometimes ask me a question about our school work. I was a stupid, little shit so I knew he didn't need my help, but I answered him anyways. Mostly, we just talked about our lives. Granted Bruce usually sat quietly while I told him about my life. He seemed so fascinated about every single detail.

On the days when Bruce would smile or talk to me, I would walk with him to an imaginary line halfway up the dirt road. Bruce would walk more quickly these days, but only to the point where we separated. I would turn around and sprint home and nine times out of ten, I marginally avoided a beating. I think Bruce knew I would walk with him regardless of whether or not I had an ambush waiting for me at home; and so he walked faster to give me the time to get home. But one day when sprinting away, I stopped and turned around to see that from that imaginary halfway mark, Bruce continued on home at such a sedate pace, it was borderline geriatric.

Soon, Bruce started meeting me on the main road on the way to school. The mornings were getting very cold and we would walk in the dark listening to the crunch of frost under our feet and watching the clouds of our breath billowing and swirling about our heads. Bruce was still wearing only his threadbare blue shirt tucked loosely into his tattered trousers. I could see the gooseflesh beneath the thin fabric and that day I stole a thick horse blanket from my uncle's barn and hid it near the road so Bruce could wear it to school. Bruce smiled at me a lot after this.

One day, when I was pushing on a bruise on my lower back, wincing while doing so, Bruce walked over to me and hugged me. I almost pushed him off because I had no idea what kind of demented notion brought this on, but at just the same moment, I had an overwhelming need to embrace him back. So I did. I put my arms around his back and squeezed gently. I felt Bruce tense up, remembering his own forgotten injuries. He pulled away quickly, but not before I felt them. Through the thin fabric of his cotton shirt, my hands passed over what could only be described as raised ridges. I could feel welts and scars of nearly identical length and thickness and we both jumped back. I stuttered and tried to ask him what happened, but he shook his head so hard it looked like it would fall off. He ran home ahead of me that day, the horse blanket left abandoned in the bole of a tree.

The next day, Bruce sat alone in the back of the classroom. I could see that he was ashen and withdrawn and he would not raise his head to look at me. I tried to talk to him but he ignored me as if I hadn't spoken. Over the weeks that followed, Bruce never spoke to me and I would walk behind him all the way to the imaginary halfway line on the dirt road. He walked slowly as he had before we became friends and I was regularly late for supper. By mid winter, I stopped following him. By spring, Bruce stopped coming to school.

One unseasonably warm afternoon in March, my mother responded with an equally uncharacteristic suggestion that we kids go outside to play. We ran from the house before she could change her mind. I ran so fast for so long that it took a while for me to realize where I was running to. Before I could stop myself, I found myself leaning up against the blistering, peeling white paint of Bruce's grandfather's farmhouse, panting and sweating.

I waited to catch my breath before moving slowly to the back side of the house, feeling along the ground with my feet to avoid a branch that could snap and give me away. I peered around the back feeling like a Soviet spy but also fully aware that I was a ridiculous child that would likely not find anything more horrifying than Bruce's grandmother in a nightgown. I inched closer to the storm window in the rear of the house, digging my toes into the cracks in the wood to boost myself high enough up to peer inside. I held my breath and quickly glanced inside. My heart rattled against my ribs so violently I was sure it was audible in the house. In the wicker chair, only mere inches from my face and separated by a thin pane of glass, were a pair of milky, vacant eyes staring right at me.

I fell backwards into the wet, decaying leaves that lay beneath the recently melted snow. I scrambled backwards on my hands, kicking up the putrefying remnants of last autumn, until my back was pressed firmly against the old maple that kept the house in perpetual shade. I rallied my courage to clamber to my feet, my legs twitching as if made of degraded rubber bands. From my vantage point set back from the house, I could make out a flattened, greasy mat of grey hair, rocking slowly in and out of my eye line. I ducked and ran back to the house, pressing my cheek against the splintering window frame. Boosting myself up again, I steeled myself to peer into the window. Her eyes were hollow and stared into the dead space behind me. My stomach dropped and I felt myself recoil, but forced myself to keep staring at her.

She couldn't see me. The elderly woman just rocked there, blindly gazing out the window at whatever it was she saw in her mind. The creaking wooden boards beneath her chair protested with every rocking motion. I stared at her only a moment longer when I heard the screams. They were muffled and at first I wasn't sure if I had imagined them because it didn't seem as though the old lady had heard them. Then, in the same slow, arthritic way that she rocked to and fro in her chair, the woman smiled.

My feet were crashing through the leaves before I knew I hit the ground, sprinting as fast as I could for the side of the house. I came to a sliding halt when I saw the storm cellar door beneath the leaves. It looked as flimsy as it did sinister. I pushed the spongy compost off the handles and saw that it was unlocked on the exterior. I lifted one door and struggled against its weight. Beginning to sweat, both from exertion and fear, the door finally succumbed to my efforts. Inside, the musty odour of the basement permeated my nostrils causing them to flair. I couldn't see anything in the dim, murkiness but the next set of screams were carried up to me as if through the percussive hallways of a stone church. It was Bruce.

I plunged into the inky blackness with reckless disregard for my own safety, stopping short of a room that was sealed with a layer of plastic sheeting. I leaned against a nearby wall and squinted to see through the hazy tarp. A tiny drop of blood obstructed my view. A whimper followed and I pushed a small corner of the sheet out of the way.

On a metal gurney like the one I saw at the hospital when Papa died, laid the small frame of a naked boy. Bruce was on his stomach with his head turned away from me, facing a clinical-looking poster of a nude, prepubescent girl. An elderly man with a violently kyphotic back leaned heavily over a tray table. He was so frail as to appear translucent, but moved in the manner of a much younger man in control of his captor.

Across Bruce's back were the scars I had felt through his shirt during our ill-fated embrace. I stared at them, trying to make sense of their uniformity, and then it dawned on me. They were tally marks. Someone had cut those into his back like notches on a bedpost. There were so many that I could only guess that they tallied to more than fifty. A fresh trail of blood ran along the curve of his scapula and pooled in the dimple of his lower back. I was about to barrel through the plastic sheeting to rescue Bruce from his tormentor, when the old man turned around.

His hair reminded me of the photos of Albert Einstein that were displayed on our classroom walls, but greasier and matted like the blind woman who smiling sadistically at the screams of a tortured boy. His face was hollow and his eyes dead. He was humming: the rumbling from his throat deep and rolling and I could make out the tune of Amazing Grace which we sang so hopefully the previous Sunday.

He held a long metal rod and without hesitation, inserted it roughly into Bruce's rectum. Bruce cried out again, clutching the sides of the gurney. The man left the rod sticking grotesquely out of his anus and returned to the tray. When he turned around, he held a barbarously large syringe with a needle that glinted in the dim light. The solution was clear and unthreatening, but when the old man flicked the plunger and let spray a small amount of it, I whimpered in fear. With a type of confidence only displayed after much practice, he injected the needle deeply into Bruce's thigh and tossed the discarded needle onto the tray.

He stood behind Bruce, obstructing my view of him. He prodded Bruce with the metal instrument and whispered something to him I could not hear.

In the clear, childlike voice you would expect to hear in a church choir, Bruce started to incant something he had evidently said many times before.

"I am a sinner. I admit to my Lord that I have committed the sin of homosexuality. I have lusted after men and for that I am being punished. Thanks for delivering me to my grandfather to administer this cure upon me. With this treatment I shall learn that my body is not that of the flesh and one day under the eyes of God I shall lay with a woman like the one before my eyes. Until that day, I will submit to the punishments I so greatly deserve."

Bruce began repeating himself. Over and over without pause. He was clearly trying to rush through it so that it would be over sooner. Then, he started shaking. At first it looked like he was shivering, but then his voice broke and he stopped talking. Soon his body began violently bucking in a monstrous fashion, snarling and smashing his face off the metal gurney. He heaved so viciously the rod that had been protruding from Bruce's orifice expelled like projectile and clambered across the stone floor. Blood wept from his wound steady as the tears that poured from his face.

Slowly his body relaxed and he turned his unseeing eyes toward me. He heaved and sighed and after what felt like an eternity, Bruce lifted his head. Without another thought, I looked around the cluttered, dingy basement room I stood in, finding a collection of old farming tools. My eyes honed in on a hack-scythe I had seen my Papa use before. It was small enough for me to swing but heavy in my shaking hands. The short blade had not seen a whetstone in years. I strode through the plastic sheeting with no real notion of what I was willing to do when I got in there.

I pushed the tarp out of my way and suddenly came face to face with the man who had just been torturing my only friend. I yelped out of shock, and a crooked smile crossed his face. I think he reached for me and without another moment's hesitation, I swung the blade in the manner I had seen crops fall at the feet of my Papa. My height was a hindrance but the momentum did not allow me to readjust or pull away. The horrific rending that I could feel through the handle when the dull, rusty blade made contact with flesh made the goosebumps spring up on my arms. I gasped, stumbled backwards and the scythe dropped from my numb fingers with a clatter.

The perverted smile that had just been smeared on Bruce's grandfather's face turned into an unhinged mouth like that of a fish upon the shore. His bowels slipped from his abdomen all at once and with a rush. The feces that oozed from the lacerate intestines splashed up my shins and I doubled over and vomited onto the pink, wet ropes at my feet. The old man let out an agonized wail and crumpled to the ground, writhing in a pool of his own innards.

I ran around him, giving an excessive berth to the dying man, and helped drag the obtunded Bruce from the gurney. I half-carried my friend into the sunlight, spurned by the guttural sounds that followed us out of the basement.

Bruce slept the whole night on the horse blanket I dug out of the tree. I had snuck away and stolen clothing, more blankets, a swath of clean cloth to use as a dressing and some food from my uncle's farm. I knew my mother would beat me to a pulp if she found out, but I wasn't going back there and Bruce was never going back either. I dressed his wounds, clothed him and curled up next to him under the stolen blankets to keep him warm.

I awoke to heaviness on my chest. It took me some moments to come to the realization that Bruce was straddling me. I tried to ask him what he was doing but it became suddenly clear that I could not speak. Two small but surprisingly strong hands encircled my throat. Bruce leaned his weight forward onto my neck until I felt the crunching of my damaged trachea.

It was still dark out, but a grey haze illuminated the horizon. I could make out Bruce's shape against the sky above me. While I could barely see because of the early dawn, the darkness began to tunnel around my vision and I knew that I was going to die. I bucked and writhed and threw my hands up into Bruce's face, clawing and scratching. He leaned back to avoid my dirty, jagged nails and released the pressure on my neck. I used this momentum to grab his arms and force him off of me. We rolled childishly around; two boys who were not quite men, comparably strong and cowardly at the same time.

After some time of grunting and struggling, I found myself straddling Bruce's chest and I could feel the weakness of the previous day's exertions seeping into his bones. Soon, I held the upper hand in which I held Bruce's arms pinned above his head and we both just remained locked in that position, sweating and panting.

Eventually, after clearing my hoarse, destroyed throat, I looked down at Bruce as he coughed and feebly kicked his legs and I croaked, "Why? I rescued you… I want to help you… Why?"

Bruce turned his tongue around in his pasty, open mouth, working up enough saliva to lubricate the words that burned in his throat. "You are the reason this has happened to me." He practically hissed at me, the words dripping with venom. "You will not live another day to inhabit my soul and penetrate me with your cock of lies!"

I almost recoiled at the words. I knew instantly that he was possessed with the poisons and the words that his grandfather injected into his malleable mind. The rage boiled behind his eyes and he made to spit at me, though nothing could come from his parched mouth. I thought that I should help him go to sleep so that he could wake up when the poisons were out of his system; and so I hit him. I lifted my hand from his wrist and struck him across the face before he could react. He winced but then turned his hateful gaze back to me as he tried to scream profanities at me. So I hit him again. He just wouldn't go to sleep. I hit him again and again and again and each time, his eyes remained open and blazing. So, on I went, striking him in the face. He stopped snarling at me and so I sat back and started to alternate hands; left and right, then left and right again. I closed my eyes when a drop of blood landed on my eyelid. It was easier to hit him when I couldn't see his face. I felt his nose break. I felt teeth fall loose from the smile I once found so beautiful. I felt a cheek become soft and wet.

It took me some time to realize that Bruce was quiet. That's when I stopped.

"ROBERT!! ROBERT!! Robert, you are safe! You are here at the Wellness Centre! You are not in the woods, Robert, you are safe!" Gnarled hands gripped my arms and shook me gently but assuredly. I shook my head to loosen the wet, crunching sounds from my ears. My gaze suddenly snapped onto the mud brown eyes framed in frizz that looked worriedly into my own.

She shushed me softly like a child coming out of a nightmare. She sat on the arm of the chair I was seated in. In an effort to comfort me, she ran her hand over my back in a compassionate gesture. She stiffened. She felt them. The tally marks.

She slowly dropped her hand and made to stand impassively, her eyes darting between me and the door. I looked up at her pityingly.

"Bruce?" Her voice quavered as she stepped backwards toward the French doors of her unassuming little office.

I stood up unhurriedly, stretching like a cat after a long nap. Frizzy Bangs staggered backwards so hard she fell onto her bony ass, taking a pile of her fucking blank notes along with her. She looked like Robert did that night under the muted dawn light. She looked like so many others since.

It was easy running away, pretending to be a troubled boy named Robert. When it was necessary, it didn't take much to be someone else for a while. I kept coming back to Robert, though. Every day and in every dream, I could see the blood in his eyes, glowing as red as the early morning sun that set the tops of the bare trees on fire. It had taken some time to realize that he had fallen quiet.

I moved slowly towards the terrified woman at my feet. "Amazing Grace, how sweet the sound/that saved a wretch like me/I once was lost, but now I'm found/was blind, but now I see," I hummed throatily.

"Yes, grandfather…it will be some time before she falls quiet, too."

Runner Up
Micky Neilson

Micky Neilson is a two-time New York Times best-selling author whose graphic novels, Ashbringer (#2 on the list) and Pearl of Pandaria (#3) have both been published in six languages. As one of the first writers at Blizzard Entertainment, he has more than two decades of experience in the cutting edge of the gaming industry. He is currently working on a graphic novel, Rook, as well as a number of film projects. In 2016 Riverdale Avenue Press published his memoir Lost and Found: An Autobiography About Discovering Family, available wherever books are sold.

http://www.mickyneilson.com

Doll Parts

MICKY NEILSON

Howard Friedkin awoke to a low, rumbling growl. The left side of his head throbbed with a dull but persistent ache. His brain was foggy. He blinked dirt from his eyes, attempting to identify the source of the noise…

A pit bull hovered just a few feet away with its head lowered, ears back, and its yellow eyes reacting to even the slightest movement; Guttural warnings rose in volume as thick slaver collected at the exposed gums of its sharply pointed yellow teeth.

From a ring on its spiked collar a tarnished chain extended, looping through another ring on the far wall, ending in a larger hoop held in the hand of…

"Well now, there he is—wake on up, Howard! You did tell me that was your name, right?"

A young woman. Twenty, if that. He remembered her now. But how did he get here? She sat against the wall, right knee up, leash in hand, her pale white arm braced inside that leg. The other leg was extended, presenting the bare, soiled bottom of her foot. Her head rested back as she glared at Howard with eyes that, aside from being dark, weren't unlike that of the pit bull.

The growl lowered to a vibrating drone as Howard risked a shaky glance at his surroundings. He was in some kind of underground room.

Or, chamber… it was like a big square chunk had been carved out of the stony ground. The walls, ceiling and floor were composed of hard-packed earth. The warped, rotted wooden door in the corner was hinged to a post that was in turn bolted into the dense soil. The space was roughly ten feet by ten feet, maybe eight feet high, illuminated by a drop light hanging from a rusted eyehook directly overhead. Its thick orange cord drooped across the ceiling to a staple where wall and ceiling met, then across and out above the top of the door.

Scattered across the floor were… doll parts. Fat, grime-coated little plastic arms and legs and bodies. Lying between the pit bull and Howard was a larger doll. Its hair was styled to look like the woman's—black, long and wiry and unkempt. It wore a dirty grey tank top and tight jean shorts, just like his captor.

"I asked you a question," she said. "Course it don't really matter what your name was."

Howard's eyes widened at the woman, who's left hand flew up, fingers covering her mouth in an "oops" gesture.

"Did I say 'was?' Well shit, I've gone and made a blunder."

Howard couldn't have answered if he wanted to: a leather strap ran between his lips, fastened behind his head, holding his jaw in an open position and keeping his tongue pinned against the bottom of his mouth. His arms were secured behind him by some kind of metal… not handcuffs, but close. Bigger. Manacles, maybe, like they used to use in medieval times. The rattle of chains accompanied the repositioning of his arms, which were sore, as was the rest of his body. Looking down, Howard realized for the first time that he was naked. Naked and covered in dirt.

The pit bull growled louder.

"Howard, or whatever your name is, I want you to do somethin' for me… I want you to use your foot, and point at that their doll, at Little Maddy…"

Maddy. That was what the woman had said her name was when he had pulled his truck up next to where she'd been standing on the street corner.

"You point that foot and show me where it was you was gonna touch me tonight," Maddy concluded.

What kind of sick game was this? Howard's guts twisted like a coiling snake.

"Go on now, get to it."

Muttering against the leather strap, Howard shook his head. All he had wanted was a little company. That wasn't so bad, was it? Now he just wanted to be anywhere but here.

Maddy swung her right leg outward, allowing the arm braced inside to move just an inch. In turn, the chain let out an inch; the pit bull drew closer, barking loudly, snapping its teeth and flinging slobber.

Howard tucked up his legs and pulled away but the restraint on his wrists held him fast.

"Rosco here likes nuts," Maddy said. "And not the kind you get in trail mix. So… let's try this again: point with your toes to where you was gonna touch me tonight."

Maddy pulled the chain back an inch. Howard extended a leg and aimed his toe at the doll's arm.

In an instant the chain came loose enough for the pit bull to reach Howard's foot. He pulled it back just as those teeth came clamping down, missing his flesh by centimeters.

Maddy leaned her head forward, yelling: "You keep bullshittin' me and see if I don't let go o' this chain! See if I don't! Now you wanna try this again?"

Howard nodded emphatically. Maddy leaned her head back.

"Show me."

His foot quavered as Howard extended it, toes hovering over the doll's chest.

Dipping her chin, Maddy smiled, satisfied. "Yeah, that's right, you was gonna play with these titties, huh?" She cupped her left breast with her left hand. Maddy wasn't wearing a bra. Under any other circumstances…

"But that ain't all, is it Howard?" Maddy's tone had taken on a sharper edge. "Show me where else."

Sweat was now coating the entirety of Howard's skin, dripping down into his eyes. He muttered a strained response. The chain slackened. Those teeth drew near, snapping and gnashing, eager to rend soft flesh.

The chain tightened. Maddy waited.

Howard extended his foot again, this time placing his toes over the doll's crotch. Maddy was nodding her head.

"That's right… that's right, you dirty fucker. That's exactly what you wanted." Her voice was low now, laced with disgust.

"I don't know why it is folks has got these problems in their brains. They got sickness in the mind. Why is that, huh?"

Maddy awaited an answer. Howard simply shook his head.

"Why people gotta be so goddamn un-Christian for?"

Howard had begun to cry now, his salty tears mingling with the sheen of salty sweat. He wondered what his chances were of making it out of this room alive.

Heavy footsteps sounded outside the chamber. Three knocks rattled the thin wooden door.

"Yeah!" Maddy shouted. The door opened…

And in walked a mountain of a man. He wore a mask, like the kind spray painters used, that covered the nose and mouth and had filters on either side. Paintball goggles with tinted lenses hid the man's eyes. Both head pieces were strapped around a massive, bald cranium with several raised scars crisscrossing its entirety.

Scars adorned the giant's shoulders and tree-trunk arms as well, disappearing beneath a set of ripped, faded overalls and a long apron… an apron stained with red liquid, some of it dried and ruddy, some of it bright and fresh.

Blood. It had to be blood. Dear Jesus.

"Brother Bones, this one's ready," Maddy said.

Workman's boots stomped across the stony ground. The behemoth produced a key from under the apron and bent down behind Howard. There was the sound of metal against metal, a key turning and then a release in the tension against Howard's arms. His wrists were still manacled, but he was no longer chained to the wall.

The masked man grabbed Howard by the neck with one meaty paw and lifted him up to his feet and against the wall away from the pit bull… and then on to the door. As he was forced out of the room, Howard heard Maddy get to her feet, heard the dog's chain rattle and stop against the ring in the wall. Rosco barked and snarled as Maddy stepped out of the chamber and around Howard and the giant she called Brother Bones.

The passageway was carved out of the same hard, pale stone-like earth, lit by more drop lights hanging overhead. The corridor wasn't wide enough for the big man and Howard to walk side by side. Brother Bones pushed Howard ahead of him with one hand, holding on to the chains and manacles that bound Howard's wrists with the other. Not being able to help himself, Howard glanced down at Maddy's ass, the folds of her cheeks peeking out from beneath the jean shorts.

When he had seen her standing on the street corner, she had been facing away, and that ass was the first thing he had seen… and he had actually thought to himself, "That there is an ass to die for."

A large opening came into Howard's view. It led to another chamber, this one much larger. Howard stopped. The opening was wide enough for three people to pass easily and afforded Howard an expansive view of what was kept inside.

Most were leaning back against the wall. A few were lying on the floor. At first Howard thought they were mannequins -- naked department store mannequins. But as he looked closer he saw, in the pale glow of the dangling work light, parts that were human. Some had the heads of men or women, and bodies of mannequins; some had the heads of mannequins and human bodies, and some… some had a mixture; a human body with mannequin arms or mannequin legs, or a mannequin body with human arms or legs… but there was one feature they all shared: the crotches were all those of a mannequin. Smooth, featureless, flesh-colored plastic.

"That there's the menagerie," Maddy said from behind Howard. "I love that word, menagerie," and there was genuine affection in her voice. "You don't go there, though. Come on…"

Brother Bones put his massive hand to Howard's head and shoved him further down the passage.

The room they came to at the end of the hall was accessed via another worn wooden door. When Howard saw the interior, just a bit larger than Maddy's menagerie, he thought he might faint. But the racing of his heart, the sheer terror that had overtaken him, kept the solace of unconsciousness at bay.

The light in here was bright and harsh, cast by standing work lamps. There were metal tables on wheels and atop the tables various surgical instruments, but mostly saws of every size and shape. Nearly the entirety of the room was coated in both wet and dry blood, as were the implements and tools. Scattered about the space, seemingly randomly, were a number of severed limbs… as well as bits and pieces of what Howard assumed was human flesh and meat. Against the wall to Howard's left was a chainsaw. Directly in front of him, almost in the center of the room, a cable dangled. At its end was a wide leather loop. The cable ran to a pulley in the ceiling, to another almost above the chainsaw, and down to a metal clip which hovered just a few feet above an eyehook set in the floor.

Maddy sauntered over to a table against the wall on Howard's right side as the giant jostled Howard to roughly the center of the room. Picking up a bloody bone saw, Maddy smiled a gap-toothed smile.

The leather noose came down around Howard's neck from behind and tightened. He bellowed against the strap in his mouth. "Like I said, you don't get to go to the menagerie. Not yet."

There was a sudden, vicious lurch as Howard's weight was lifted off the floor. His feet kicked futilely. Garbled noises and spit flew from his mouth. He heard the click of the clip behind him.

Maddy wiped blood off the blade with one finger. "See, that area you pointed to on the doll that second time, where you was gonna touch me? That's where Brother Bones is gonna touch you. And then, then you get to go to the menagerie."

The last sound Howard heard was the high whine of the chainsaw motor.

Runner Up
Victoria Griffin

After earning her BA in English from Campbell University, Victoria returned to her East Tennessee roots. She is a freelance writer and editor, a teller of dark tales, and a peanut-butter addict. Her short fiction is set to appear in A Journey of Words and Incandescent Mind, among others.

www.VictoriaGriffinFiction.com

www.facebook.com/victoriagriffinfiction

Vodka Memories

VICTORIA GRIFFIN

The textured ceiling twisted like wax in a lava lamp above Melanie as she stretched out on her bare mattress. Her sheets were still packed in egg crates downstairs and would smell like cardboard for a month. She didn't even have a blanket to cover up with, but the vodka in her stomach kept her warm.

She heard the door slam downstairs, and she smiled. Danny had sat alone for nearly an hour in the empty living room, presumably staring at the empty walls and thinking about the way the Grey Goose had tasted on her lips. He had bought it, of course. All her money was tied up in the down payment for this place, but it was worth it to get away from that goddamn apartment that had trapped her for the last eight years. That tiny closet of a place with an oven that couldn't open completely without hitting the cabinets and an ironing board that folded out of the wall. She hated that apartment—the thin walls, the stained carpet, the roommate.

Danny didn't believe her the night she told him that Tiffany was standing outside her room, listening to them have sex. He laughed and kissed her ear even though he knew she hated that. She remembered the churning in her stomach as Danny moved his lips over her hip, and she watched the two shadows still beneath the crack of the bedroom door. Just a trick of the light. She's not a pervert, after all. She's an elementary school teacher.

It was right after she broke up with Danny the second time—he'd used her good slow cooker to strip paint off old door hinges—that Melanie found the book. She was sifting through Tiffany's bookshelf, trying to find out whether she already owned the novel she'd bought her for Christmas, when she touched the leather journal. The binding was softer than even Melanie's vintage leather boots. She tipped the journal from the shelf and glanced around Tiffany's room before opening it. The pages were dark, almost black, and covered in white lettering. She had never seen white ink make marks so opaque, but she had never seen marks like these either. There were no letters from the Latin alphabet, no numbers or even wingdings characters. They were sharp lines, not really connecting, not forming shapes, just scattered sporadically over the ash-colored pages.

When she heard Tiffany's key fiddling in the lock, Melanie crammed the book between two thick volumes and bolted out of the room, twisting her body so she appeared to be coming out of her own.

Melanie imagined those jagged, white marks connecting the shadows on the popcorn ceiling. She hadn't told Danny about the journal, but she hadn't told him about the day Leo disappeared either. Her hand fell over the edge of the bed, her fingers caressing the soft mattress topper. She could still feel Leo's curly hair, the slight depressions in his cheeks from childhood acne. She could lose herself in the memory of his pale green eyes. When he'd leaned in to kiss her, all she'd seen was green. All she'd felt was green. Soothing like a field of fine, spring grass.

Danny knew that she had dated Leo, and he knew that she'd loved him. Danny probably also knew that she had loved Leo more than she could ever love him. He knew that Melanie had cried herself to sleep on the floor, then in her bed, then in Danny's arms. He knew that she had put her box of forget-me-nots in storage because she couldn't stand the sight of the necklace Leo had given her or the newspaper clipping from their first concert together.

Danny knew all about her past with Leo and about the future they should have had together. But he didn't know what had happened right before he'd disappeared. Danny wouldn't believe it meant anything, that it was connected to Leo at all. But Melanie knew, and her knuckles stiffened thinking about that morning.

The sun was already bright through the windows as Melanie padded out of her room in a sports bra and pajama pants. Tiffany stood with her back to the kitchen sink, looking out the living room window at the half-full parking lot. Her hands were crooked claws at her sides, and her white hair dripped into the small of her back. (Melanie had never believed her when she said she didn't dye it, but she believed her now.) Her eyes were trained on something outside the apartment.

"Are you waiting for someone?" Melanie dropped a dish in the sink behind her roommate, but Tiffany didn't move. "It's only nine. Most people are still in church."

Tiffany's red lip twitched, but she didn't speak. She hated church. So did Melanie, but she supposed having a preacher-father whip her every other night gave her the right. She watched her roommate, cinching her brows, but Tiffany didn't move. Melanie took a bottle of water and started toward her room. Leo would pull up in his blue Nissan soon, and she wanted to look nice for brunch.

"He's not coming."

Melanie paused with her back to Tiffany, the open water bottle halfway to her lips. "What?"

"Leo's not coming. Don't bother getting dressed."

Melanie turned to find Tiffany in the same position, staring at the same fixed place somewhere outside. "Did he call?"

No answer.

"Well, how do you know he's not coming?"

Tiffany closed her eyes and sank into the fetal position on the tile floor. Melanie wanted suddenly to kick the white-haired girl until her face was bloody and her skinny torso was raw.

She thought of the leather journal, its dark pages, and something stopped her.

Melanie walked into her room and closed the door, chugged the water like it was vodka, and dolled up her face for the love of her life, whom she would never see again.

The mattress shook under her back, and the ceiling was still twirling like ribbons in a little girl's hair. Melanie rolled halfway onto her side, felt the bile pushing up her throat, but she didn't puke. Grey Goose was too expensive. She ran her palm over the mattress, petting it like a cat. The open closet gaped at her.

The police had found the blue Nissan a week after their broken date. Someone had called in an anonymous tip that had led them straight to the car, stuffed in the forest off a dirt road used only by fishermen. Leo had been in the back seat, smelling like a raccoon in an old bear trap. He'd had no markings, no wounds, no drugs or alcohol in his system. He was just dead.

Melanie had beat the walls of the goddamn apartment, nearly torn the place down. She'd thrown skillets at the doors and had broken the windows with bloody fingers. Danny broke the door down one evening and sped her to the hospital just in time to pump the sleeping pills from her stomach.

Tiffany had been silent. She'd dressed in black and didn't leave her room. She'd frowned, but she'd never cried.

Melanie's doctors had prescribed anti-depressants. She'd taken mild sedatives before the funeral. Danny had held her hand and propped her up in the pew. After they'd all viewed the body and hugged Leo's mother and listened to the preacher's sermon, Danny had taken Melanie aside and told her what the coroner had found clutched in Leo's hand—a ring.

Through her tears and drug-dulled hysteria Melanie had not noticed Tiffany standing near them, her arms folded over her black silk dress.

Melanie rolled onto her stomach, feeling the mattress shift beneath her tiny frame. She had lost weight recently, which is why the Grey Goose hit her so hard. Danny was worried. He said she needed to go back to therapy, start taking medication again, use diet supplements. He had been nagging her about it tonight—too many martinis and not enough food. Too much television and not enough exercise.

"I'm fine, Danny." She tipped a martini glass full of straight vodka down her throat and chased it with an olive from the tray on the coffee table.

"You're not fine, and we both know it. You're sick, Melanie, and you need to get help. You know I just want to see you healthy because I love you."

"Don't say that, Danny."

"Don't say what?"

"You know what."

"Melanie, I love—"

"Stop it, Danny."

"Just because you loved Leo doesn't mean you can't ever love again."

She stood up from the couch. He put a hand out to steady her, but she knocked it away before grabbing the bottle and emptying it on her way up the stairs. She tossed it over her shoulder and listened to it shatter against the hardwood.

Then she collapsed on her bed. Watched the ceiling spin. Stared into the closet's dark mouth. The mattress shifted beneath her.

Melanie thought about Leo, touched the inside of her thigh like he might have. Then she thought about her would-be fiancé dead in the back of his Nissan. Thought about the ring in his cold fingers. Thought about Tiffany standing outside the bedroom door, staring out the window, crouched on the tile the day he didn't come back. Melanie rolled onto her stomach and put her hands beneath her chest, her palms flat against the sheet, and clawed at the mattress as though digging in dirt. She bit her pillow and let the hot tears roll down the pillowcase onto her lips. Her nails dug into the soft mattress—then broke through.

The covering of the mattress ripped, and her fingers plunged into it as though it were rotten fruit. She jerked her chest upward, and her entire fists disappeared so that she was elbow-deep in the mattress. She rolled onto her hips, trying to dislodge her arms, but they were caught at the wrists. Her legs flailed as she sank deeper, her shoulders pressed into the rotten material, her nose crammed into the pillow, still smelling of salty tears.

It was only an itch at first. A small tingle crawling gently along the vein on the inside of her wrist. It made its way up to her elbow, then into her shoulder socket, before traveling the length of her spine and settling in her tailbone. Then another started in her wrist, stronger. And on the other side. Like insects inside her skin.

She jerked her arms again, but whatever held her wrists stayed fast, and the tingling sensation strengthened and spread over her skin, around her arms, down her back, and around her neck like a tight noose. Her body contorted, bent backward like a howling dog, and she screamed. Her voice cracked in desperate pain—the same way she had imagined Leo's voice to have sounded as he'd died in the back seat of his Nissan.

Her wrists came free, and she fell across the bed onto the floor, her limbs in a tangle. The lights flickered on, and she saw hundreds of insects in a trail between her and the bed, like black centipedes with giant pincers. Her limbs flailed like the insects' scuttling legs as she scrambled backward across the floor until her back struck the wall. She felt her ribs rattle within her, and her heart used her lungs like punching bags.

Her skin was moving. Long, thin bulges traveled the length of her arms. She pulled up her shirt and saw them moving over her stomach, like rippling abdominal muscles. She felt them in her back and all over her legs. At the base of her spine and in the tips of her toes. Crawling, crawling.

It felt like the static in an empty television channel, consuming her mind and pressing on her like cotton balls stuffed behind her eardrums. She covered her face with her palms—and saw the holes. There were bloody circles on her wrists, as though made with a screwdriver. As she held her shaking hands in front of her, one of the insects crawled over her palm and into the hole in her wrist, disappearing beneath her skin.

She tried to scream, but her vocal cords snapped like gnawed licorice. She tried to stand, but her ankles collapsed—the bones were eaten through like casu marzu. Her body crashed back down to the floor, and she felt the Grey Goose spill through her stomach, the lining half-eaten away. The vodka flooded her insides, drowning some of the creatures and lighting her vision with red flashes. Her jaw was settled hard against the wood, and she let the pain overtake her, beating through her skull and into her mind and destroying every shred of herself.

A hole formed just above her bellybutton. Black insects cascaded out, chased by Grey Goose vodka. They circled her still body until they found her wrists, entered again, and made their way to her brain, where they punched holes in every memory she had.

When Melanie's heart finally stopped beating, she did not remember Danny or Tiffany or Leo. She knew nothing except pain, not even her name. When her writhing body grew still, the insects found their way out through her nose and her eyes. They crawled up the bedframe and into the mattress, leaving her corpse twisted on the floor.

Tiffany did not cry at Melanie's funeral. She frowned with red lips, and her pale hand sat crooked against the black material of her dress like white lettering on a black page.

Runner Up

Chevoque

Chevoque was born in Klerksdorp, South Africa, and as an only child, the world seemed like a lonely place, until she set her mind free and got lost in the worlds she created for herself.

Authors Website - http://goo.gl/AQaK6J

https://www.facebook.com/ChevoquePublic/

Escape the Darkness

CHEVOQUE

There was an eerie darkness to the world, after everything had changed a few days ago. What had changed, she wasn't certain, but she was searching for the answers, as she knew only one thing: she had lost him completely.

She stands staring at the photo; her own smile was hopeful and her friend or lover's was equally joyful. For a moment, she tries remembering something. Anything. She knows she loved him, but she can't remember why or how it had happened.

The staircase in front of her, creaks, but she ignores it. The house is old and nothing seems strange anymore. Even the muffled voices, talking in the walls, seem normal at this stage. She hears that voice again, and in her mind she is certain it is the Devil's, but she has never done much wrong and the voice just continues speaking in a language with which she is not familiar.

Taking the first few steps, she stops at a photo of him and his friends. She recalls everyone and knows her relationship with each, but still she doesn't know what her relationship was with him. Who is he? She ponders.

Daniel, she knew his name was Daniel and that this is his house. Is this his house? She becomes uncertain, as she stares at the photo. She has seen it a million times, but things have changed; she now looks at everything differently since...she can't remember since when. She just knows something is different and it makes her skin crawl. She feels a breath on her neck and hears the soft whispers in the walls, but again, she ignores it.

At the top of the staircase she hears someone sigh. This time she turns to look and there he is. It's Daniel, standing in a suit, holding the watch she gave him for Christmas in his hands. A tear escapes from his eye and drops onto the watch. He wipes it away with his thumb and she takes another step closer to comfort him.

Suddenly, he disappears; like an evaporating cloud he is gone and her heart burns with the pain, but she still can't remember what her relationship was with him. What was he to her and she to him?

Something inside her tells her they were lovers, but the muffled voices in the walls deny it and the Devil whispers in her ear, "Love is pain."

Startled, she runs up the last few steps and stares down, but no one is there. She is alone in the dark house, where the only light is coming from Daniel's room. She needs to go there and get something; she isn't sure what it is, but she follows the flicker in the darkness.

As she passes the first room, she hears a soft cry downstairs. Looking over the handrail, she sees Daniel standing at the table next to the staircase. He takes his car key and shoves it into his pocket and looks up. He seems to look right at her and says, "I wish you understood, Scary." Again, he dissolves like a perfume cloud that permeates the air.

Scary was his nickname for her. She is Scarlet and he was Daniel.

Is that what happened to him? she asks herself. Did he die in a car accident? And what was I supposed to understand? She continues her route toward his room. The light, streaming into the hallway is that tungsten yellow colour. He liked them more than the energy saver type; the thought comes to her mind, as she enters.

It is clearly a guy's room, but it felt comfortable. The plasma screen against the wall has a cabinet beneath it filled with numerous gaming consoles. There is a photo of them on his nightstand and it was from when they had their first Christmas together. This nearly convinces her that they had to be lovers, but that voice, the Devil's, teases her once more with indistinguishable words.

She takes the photo and hugs it tightly against her chest. It is as if she felt something for the first time in days, so she cries, as the emotions overwhelm her. Minutes pass as she sits on the bed hugging the photo. She stays confused and desperately seeks the answers she struggles to find.

Her first tears escape; she sees a flash of red and hears the yell of a woman. She passes out and lies on the bed, momentarily lost in her haunted mind.

"Oh, my lost little soul, you need to see," the Devil whispers in the back of her mind, as the walls laugh at her. With a flashing image she sees the streets run red with blood and this has her convinced that Daniel must have died in a car accident.

When she wakes up again, she looks down -- down into a grave, down at a casket. She looks around her -- people dressed in black surround her. Daniel is next to her mother, comforting her. Her father stands in the distance, a whiskey bottle wrapped in brown paper bag in his hand.

Why would my parents…? Then it all comes back, as she sees that the first person throwing a black rose onto the casket is her mother.

She had it all wrong! She is the one who has died!

She'd died in Daniel's house and he wasn't on his way to his own death, he was coming here, here where she is now to remain…forever. She panics and tries drawing his attention. She jumps up and down in front of him; she tries grabbing her mother's shoulders to wake her up and shouts until her lungs burn, just to draw some attention, but nothing happens.

"No, my lost little soul," the Devil sounds nearly bereft, as he speaks to her. "You have been lost in the darkness because of how you died… because of how you gave your soul to me when you died. Because of what you are."

"No!" she shouts and tries cowering behind Daniel, as she searches for the origin of the Devil's voice.

"I'm in your veins. You can't exist without me from here on forward." Scarlet tries denying it. She tries fighting the memories filling her dark mind. "This is your goodbye. Remember, my lost little soul, remember, so I might take you home."

"I am home! I am where I must be! I didn't die! You are trying to win my soul!" She shouts and in an instant she is back in Daniel's house. She has no control, as her body leads her to his room. Again and again.

"Stop fighting and face it!" the Devil commands the sixth time she avoids the truth by making the memory loop in her mind. He boils in her blood, blurs her vision and she finally enters. Daniel was having sex with another girl, a girl Scarlet knew was his girlfriend, but she never wanted to accept that he never wanted her the way she wanted him.

She never understood that they couldn't be. He had told her time after time, but she was stubborn, she was hopeful and she got hurt. She had run away when he saw her standing in the doorway.

Daniel and her parents couldn't find her for two days and no one knew where Scarlet had gone, but on the 6th of June 2006, she'd entered his home after he had left. She'd gone straight up to his room and moved the furniture so she could draw a pentacle in the middle of the room. After placing five candles at each designated area, she sat down in the middle, drew the gun from the bag and recited some Latin words she had found online.

"You make it too easy, my lost little soul," the Devil had whispered into her ear even before she brought the gun closer to load it. She only felt the shiver, but didn't hear his words above her own voice reciting the ancient curse.

She found that the only way she would ever have Daniel for herself, was if she was to curse him to never find love again and her life, her sacrifice, was the ultimate price she was willing to pay. She placed the gun against her cheek, as the curse drew to an end.

"I love you, Daniel," she'd said and pulled the trigger.

Again, the flash of red dominated her sight and the street - where she always dreamt of her white picket fence with Daniel - ran red with her blood.

She looks onto the scene; her mother running in and yelling at the sight. Blood was splattered against the white candles and one was extinguished; showing the curse had been successful, as the circle had been broken when she died.

"My lost little soul, you gave your payment," the Devil cunningly says in her mind.

"This isn't real," she looks confusedly onto the scene, almost fast forwarding towards the point where Daniel sat on his bed one last time, before heading to the memorial service. He holds the photo of them and pleads, but she can't hear his words. She only hears muffled voices in the walls, muffled voices leaving her grave, before her last inspiration hits and she is back at her grave.

"You were so lost, Scary. We couldn't save you. You should have understood that we couldn't be together." The gentleness in Daniel's voice gives way and he speaks more sternly. "You couldn't have understood. I know that now, but you are my sister. What the fuck was wrong with you? You really were the Devil's child, as father said. You probably faked that he touched you and caused him to get in trouble for nothing! At least now you are where you belong...in Hell!"

Scarlet stands staring, as her brother spits on her casket, but then the flaming hand that envelops hers, fuses her to the Devil. "Come, you have a new family whose faith needs breaking."

She looks at her hand and her veins turn black. They run up her arm and soon her eyes turn the shade of darkness and emptiness, and she remembers exactly what she is. She smiles at her Master, as it all comes back and the world turns to flames, as she transforms into a newborn baby. The flames break into a yellow hospital nursing room, as her sacrificed soul is placed over a pure baby sleeping in a cradle.

A cry of a burning soul and the sizzle of innocence is heard in the inter-dimension, before the baby smiles at the Devil, which gives the baby his mark. It is a birthmark where the bullet had entered Scarlet's cheek and the new cycle begins.

Runner Up

Andrea Merchak

I'm from Brazil and recently found out I really enjoy writing. I love horror stories, especially the gory ones, full of violence, crossed by taboos and scary vicious characters. Stephen King inspires my writing. I've published one novel (Bloody Legends) so far, and others are in process in my mind.

Authors Blog - http://bit.ly/1pXFHok

Twitter - @AndieMerchak

Deadly Senses

ANDREA MERCHAK

It's been a year today since the Japanese created a program that allows the transmission of the five senses through electronic means. Everyone thinks it's amazing to watch a program on TV or computer, on their cellphone or on a tablet and feel as if they are actually there, whatever is being broadcast.

Although I'm only 19 years old, I have a PhD degree in IT and work in one of the largest Information Technology companies in the world. However, even having already proven how highly worthy I am on several occasions, because of my young age and proven genius, I am still victim of some kind of abuse.

I had been working on a personal venture similar to the project developed by the Japanese and they just helped me finish my program much earlier than I expected. My program allows me to manipulate people to do exactly what I want through one of their senses and hence self-inflict devastating damage to themselves. And the best of it is that it cannot be detected as the effects could be considered either accidental or suicide attempts.

So, I decided to make better use of technology and use my program to show, once and for all, that I will not tolerate any abuse anymore. And even being so young, I have a long list of abusers. However, I gave the issue some thought and decided: five senses, five inductees.

*****

I'll start with John Roberts. A stupid guy at least five years older than I am, who used to beat me, push me against the lockers at school or throw me to the ground. He perpetrated all sorts of physical abuse against me with those rough hands of his. I wanted to see how he would feel when the situation is reversed.

Ryan and Mark were always with him, and, although they never assaulted me, they were not mere viewers. They praised the violence John inflicted on me. So it is only fair that they also participate in my revenge in the same way.

I hacked their PCs and found out that they usually meet in a virtual place where gamers connect to play online. They especially love the Kick All Asses, in which the goal is to fight against one another until the winner defeats every opponent. The best thing is that they use Kinect to play.

Because of this new technology, for this type of interactivity in which physical contact can cause damage to health, there is a security safeguard and the game limits the intensity of the blows. It even locks the game when the player reaches a certain number of blows received in specific areas of the body that would be considered dangerous.

At the beginning, I allowed the three of them to play freely. Then, gradually, I started releasing the locking parameters so that they would begin to feel more intensively the blows from physically stronger players.

The astonishment in their faces was unsurpassed. But I couldn't lose the focus and the final match had to be between John, Ryan and Mark. And they celebrated the result enthusiastically.

As soon as the fight started, I immediately deactivated several movements of John's Kinect, including tapping out. And I also disabled some security lockers. The first punches and kicks against him had already weakened him. And despite being surprised, Ryan and Mark wouldn't miss the opportunity and would attack him as hard as they could.

The more John lost his strength, the harder Ryan and Mark attacked. The two teamed up against him and, as expected, they had no idea that they were beating him beyond what he could bear, confident in the safety lockers the game usually offered.

As the slaughter continued, I kept encouraging the two to kick his ass as they used to do with me, even though they could not hear me.

I could hear the crack of his bones, the spurting of his blood and yet his two opponents didn't stop. And when they finally realized that John wouldn't move anymore, they turned against each other to finish the fight. That's only when they were able to realize what they just done because the game safety lockers had been turned off.

Ryan and Mark disconnected from the game, called 911 and rushed to John's home. But it was too late. He died from the beating he took. He had been defeated by the hands of his best friends, who would now have to live the rest of their lives knowing that they killed him.

*****

Abigail Woods is a famous painter now. And this woman's arrogance has no limits. She used to tease me in college saying that I spent so much time studying that I smelled like the mothballs used to prevent bookworms.

Technology today uses mercury, lead, beryllium and cadmium in parts of computers, cell phones, screens, batteries etc. Prolonged exposure to these tainting materials causes huge damage to health, including cancer and nervous system decay.

Although she was always exposed to paints and paint thinners, she'd never had enough exposure of these chemicals to actually be damaging enough, as far as I'm concerned!

I sent her a strong odor of mothballs through her cell phone and made her keep her face very close to the device, so that while she was breathing, she was forced to inhale whatever came out of her cell.

At the same time, I hacked an electronics manufacturer system and started a fire of great proportions. As the metals burned, they started being released and I transmitted the gases to Abigail's mobile, and she had no choice but to inhale that overly contaminated air.

A day later, Abigail was found by an assistant and quickly taken to the hospital. In addition to quivering, she had dementia and nervous system decay. In the future, a cancer may develop in her lungs, but from now on she will have a vegetative life.

*****

Joe Gibson worked as a janitor in the same company as I do. Despite being fat, every time he walked by me, he had the urge to use derogatory nicknames related to the fact I am thin. To add insult to this, he also had the guts to pick up leftovers he got when he was doing the cleaning and place them on my workstation.

At the beginning, my co-workers found that amusing, but after a while they said that I should forget about it, because he's probably frustrated or intimidated by my intelligence, youth and elegance. But I don't think that I should have had to put up with it.

Since he was so fond of eating, my choice was easy. Joe worked the night shift and he usually listened to music on his mobile while he's working. I sent him the idea to get all products that have caustic soda in their formula to fill his work cart.

I monitored his mobile GPS and waited until he came to the area of the meeting rooms that are usually empty by then. Then I made him display all the products on the table as if it were a banquet. After that, I told him to sit down and start savouring them.

I researched the reactions to caustic soda intake, so I could follow up what was going on with Joe. After ingesting, the person experiences a burning feeling, so I made him choose taking the liquid products in order to relieve the burning reaction. The pain caused by the chemical burn is severe and, besides affecting the mucous membrane of the mouth and throat, the esophagus is the most affected area.

Joe uttered desperate cries of pain, but he couldn't resist following my commands and he kept swallowing the products until he passed out. Or perhaps he died then -- I don't know for sure. The next morning, when he was found in front of the cleaning products displayed like a banquet on the huge conference table, everybody thought he had committed suicide.

*****

Emma Hallowell is very beautiful and a trainee in the company where I work. But she is as beautiful as she is incompetent. She's always very charming to everyone so that we guys help her with something, and in the end, we end up by doing the entire job for her. I myself did it several times.

Of course I knew Emma did it with everyone and it was part of her appeal. But she always had a special way of talking to me; she was even affectionate when she addressed me as "my gorgeous skinny".

So, one day I was bold enough to make a move and invited her on a date. She declined, saying she'd love to but that she had a boyfriend. I thought it was a convincing excuse and accepted it. But at the cafeteria later that day, I heard Emma telling three co-workers an "ugly as hell walking skeleton" like me had had the nerve to invite someone like her, "so wonderfully beautiful" on a date. She said she could hardly bear to look at my ugly face and the only thing I was good for was to do her work for her.

A few days later I made a video call to Emma. Within minutes I realized that she wanted to dismiss me. While she was talking to me, I sent her a signal to make her feel like turning on her PC screen.

As soon as Emma was facing the screen, I made her fix her gaze on it and began to broadcast an image of the sun shining brightly, continuing to make it more and more intense until the effect was the same as if she were looking directly at the sun itself.

I made her unable to look away and all she could do was scream while the extremely bright light burned her retina. Hopefully she remembered that I was the last image she saw before becoming blind.

*****

George Lennon is a mediocre musician who unfortunately happens to be my neighbour. We live in semi-detached houses and the room where he decided to make his studio is right next to my bedroom. He rehearses extensively throughout the night regardless of my desire to sleep.

I had made several complaints because of the noise, but every time he argued that I was lucky to be the first to hear his songs before he got famous. And as soon as he arrived home, he resumed the torture. And, believe me, when I say that even if that noise was good, the volume was so absurdly high that it was only an unbearable blast.

I was late at work because I wanted to be as far away as possible from that hideous sound. I knew the time he'd start the pseudo rehearsal. I connected and started my program. All equipment pieces that could produce sound in that room were turned on. I intensified the volume at least 10 times the maximum decibels bearable to the human ear.

I can't be sure whether he screamed, but for the first time in years, I could sleep soundly surrounded by the most wonderful and absolute silence. And from now on, since George had his eardrums burst by the very high sound, he will never bother me again.

*****

I feel refreshed now. To celebrate, I decided to buy a special wine.

As I don't know anything about liquors, I asked the guy at the store if he could give me a hint about some good wine. He was very rude and very aggressive, and said, "children are not allowed to drink." The guy didn't even bother to ask my age.

I may be young for many things, but there is no scientist in the world, young or old, with my power.

I will upgrade my program. I'll make it possible to use one or more or all of the senses combined with the ability to influence any abuser to suffer physical and/or mental fatal damage.

I will provide the program in the form of a virus so that people like me who are discriminated against just for being different from most individuals can avenge all evil caused to them.

*****

A year ago I released the virus. I totally lost control and now the world's population is no more than a few million. I cannot figure out why the remaining humanity must live apart from any kind of technology.

Those who insist on using technology or, like me, are researching for ways to reverse the chaos that the world is experiencing, are limited to a few minutes using safeguards to try to cheat the system without being hit by it.

For those who cannot manage to escape, the only option offered is to undergo the most terrible experiences before their imminent death.

Runner Up
Michaela Turcotte

Michaela Turcotte lives in Hamilton, Ontario where she is studying Journalism. She has been reading books since the age of 2, novels since age 4, and writing since she was able to hold a pen. This is her first publication.

Oblivion

MICHAELA TURCOTTE

My heart was beating so rapidly I was afraid that I was verging on a heart attack. Fear consumed me as I continued down the long, dark corridor. Everything felt damp and exposed. I heard a shriek from behind me and whirled around, but all I could see was the black emptiness of the cave. I turned back and ran. This stupid tunnel had to end eventually and I was going to get out. I didn't know how I got here, or how I would get out, but that didn't mean I wouldn't try. I kept running and was suddenly glad for my training. Waking up for track at five o'clock every morning had never felt as good as it did now. I ran and it seemed as though nothing was changing, until the dimmest of lights appeared at the end of the tunnel. I kicked in an extra burst of speed and ran straight into the light, which seemed to solidify as I reached it. I felt myself knocked back, the breath knocked out of me, and my eyes flew open.

I was in my bedroom now. My lungs welcomed the sudden burst of air, and I lay panting on the mattress, which was soaked with my sweat. I pulled myself into a sitting position and hunched over the edge of the bed. Standing, I made my way over to my dresser to look in the mirror. The mirror. The mirror over my dresser was gone. I lifted my left hand in front of me, and seven fingers danced in front of my eyes. My heart burst into a panic. I was not awake.

I clenched my eyes shut and focused all of my attention on waking myself up, to no avail. I raced down the stairs into the kitchen and over to the sink, running the water as cold as it would go, then sticking my face directly under the stream. It covered my face, running off of it, but I didn't feel a thing. I didn't feel cold, or wet, because it wasn't real. None of this was real.

My eyes shot open. I was back in my bedroom. I shifted my eyes instantly to the dresser where the mirror was intact. I tried to lift my arm to check my fingers, but it wouldn't move. I tried my other arm. Nothing. Suddenly, I felt a pressure on my chest. A crushing, immobilizing pressure, as if someone had placed a box full of bricks directly on top of me. My breathing became short and quick and I focused my mind on every individual muscle in my body, begging something to move. A black form found its way to the corner of my bedroom and I began to cry, desperately trying to fight the paralysis. Then it appeared.

Let me be clear, this was not the first time that this had happened, and if I made it out alive, I was sure it would not be the last. But my life hung on a thread every single time, and it never became easier. I was prone to lucid dreaming. I was prone to sleep paralysis. This meant that while my dreams were completely in my control, my waking life sometimes wasn't. You may know that if you die in a dream, you also die in real life. I didn't want to die. Which also meant that it was up to me to steer my dreams away from danger. Every night was a battle. I was thoroughly convinced that there was some kind of evil entity sharing my bedroom, but science explained that away. It was the only thing doctors, psychologists, psychiatrists, therapists and councillors refused to help me with, even though I was sure if we could eliminate that threat, the rest of my problems would follow suit. But it was back.

The thick black form began to take shape at the floor, a swirling plume of smoke building up and eventually solidifying into a solid mass. I fought every instinct I had in me to force my body to move, just the smallest bit, and failed miserably. The shape didn't seem to have edges, but shimmered, and began to move towards my bed, where I was trapped. I pulled on the muscles of my jaw, begging it to open, to let me scream, but it didn't budge. I tried the last part of my body that I thought I could control, my eyelids. I slid them closed, thankful that they moved, took a deep breath, and did everything I could to will the being away. I slowly opened my eyes to a black smoke cloud disappearing before me, and my body broke free of the invisible restraints. I sat straight up and looked immediately towards my window. Light. One more night behind me.

Getting out of bed was exhausting. I pulled on some sweats and shuffled down the stairs where both my parents were waiting in the kitchen with bright smiles and warm coffee.

"How'd you sleep, honey?" my father asked, already dressed for work. I plastered on as much of a smile as I could muster.

"Good," I said simply. I was heavily medicated at night. I'd been switched to different meds so many times that I didn't even really know what I was on now, but it was supposed to make it stop. After the fifth time, I realized medication wasn't the problem, and neither was my mind, and I stopped telling people it wasn't working. I would have to deal with this on my own, and today was the day I would do that. I grabbed an apple from the centre of the table.

"There's a field trip today that I forgot to sign up for," I told them. "My whole grade is going to be out of class, so I'm just gonna stay home, if that's cool." My parents exchanged a weary look, but I knew it wouldn't be an issue.

"Alright, hon, but no naps," My mother instructed firmly. I nodded, took a firm bite from my apple, and hopped back up the stairs.

So, what did you wear to an appointment like this? I decided on jeans and a red hoodie, tossing my hair up in a quick bun. I didn't think this was the kind of place I had to worry about my appearance. I sat in my desk chair, still a little too shaken to go back to my bed, and flipped through a text book, waiting to be sure my parents were gone and not returning. When the digital clock on my desk told me it was eleven o'clock, I made my way downstairs, out the door, and to the bus stop. Riding the bus, my heart felt as though it were beating in my throat. With my mind containing my fear and curiosity, there was almost not enough of my attention left to contain the vomit rising in my throat. My stomach churned at every bump, but I managed to keep myself in one piece, until I finally hopped off. The bus let off directly in front of the building I would be entering, and looking up at it, I felt an intense thrumming of my heart and lungs, doubled over, and puked on the sidewalk.

The sickness was an intense, but short-lived hell, and I'd wiped my mouth and was heading inside within minutes. I wasn't sure if I should knock, but decided against it and walked right in. The building smelled of dust and lavender. The smell wasn't necessarily unpleasant, but it was strong, and it irritated my already nervous and upset stomach. The walls were tall and beautiful, almost Victorian in design. Paintings by all kinds of artists and of many different subjects hung over a dark, old-style wallpaper. A lush red carpet gave beneath my feet, and the accents of the house were gold. Everything was immaculately clean, which I didn't expect. Then they came.

I'd taken only a few steps down the main corridor when two women appeared at the end, coming around the corner to greet me.

"Hi," I started before they made it to me. "I--" one of the women held up a hand. I stopped talking immediately. Something about disobeying them terrified me.

"We know," the woman said in a deep voice. "Take us there." My heart sped. I wasn't entirely sure what she meant, but I wasn't sure I could summon the courage to ask. The only thing I could think of is that they wanted to see my room, so I took a deep breath, and decided just to start walking.

Let me tell you, riding the bus with two members of a Wiccan coven was easily the most uncomfortable and strange experiences of my life. It seemed only to become more awkward by the minute, and I was thankful when it ended, and I was able to walk them into my house and lead them up to my room.

As we made our way down the hallway to my room, one of the woman stepped quickly in front of me and slammed a hand against my chest, stopping my movement. I froze. The other witch continued on ahead of us and pointed to my door.

"This room?" she asked simply, and I nodded quickly and silently. She gave a slower nod.

"I feel," she said, before beckoning her sister forward with a simple wave of her fingertips. She looked back at me. "You stay."

Part of me was aware of the fact that I was letting two strangers not only into my house, but into my room alone, but it didn't matter. This was my last hope. The witches went into my room, and closed the door behind them. Fear and impatience overtook my body with every passing minute. I could have sworn that it was hours before they emerged, but it was hardly five minutes when they came out and pulled their heads back to motion me in. My hands and knees were shaking and I forced my feet to take me forward. They shut the door behind me. I looked at the two women as they stared at each other, seeming to communicate silently. They both turned to me.

I looked at them both and realized then that the two of them were a sort of blur in my mind. Regardless of the fact that they looked nothing alike, I couldn't seem to differentiate them in my head. The first of them stepped forward, and placed a hand on my arm. I felt instantly comforted as a sense of peace overtook me. A small voice in the back of my head warned me that she could be altering my moods somehow, but mostly they made me feel safe. She spoke.

"We need your help with this part.," she said, her voice gentle. She knew I was afraid, and I appreciated her efforts to keep me feeling safe and comfortable. "We need you to sleep."

The words sunk in. I looked at her and felt the world begin to spin around me. The sick feeling came back to my stomach and I couldn't seem to focus on my surroundings. Sleep? Without any medicated help, without any barriers, without anything to stop myself from falling? Sleep. I tried to look at their faces, but my body felt as though it was being pulled apart, and I couldn't force it together to work the way it was supposed to. I had to trust them. I backed towards the bed, feeling my way there, still disoriented. I lay down on my back and looked at them, fear paralyzing me. I found the obscure blobs of their faces, and kept my vision glued there. I took a deep breath as I saw what I was sure was one bone-white hand sweep over me, closed my eyes, and then I was in darkness.

When I opened my eyes, I was in my room still, but the witches were gone. I was alone. I looked around the room and everything seemed normal. Did they leave? I tried to pull myself off the bed, and felt the familiar thick glue of paralysis pressing me to the pillow. Then the crushing weight on my chest. I let out a loud gasp, part scream, and tried to fight the pain. The room around me quickly blackened, and that was all there was: a thick blackness in which I was surrounded and a crushing weight on my chest. I wondered if perhaps I was going blind, maybe even dying, and then I saw myself. Lying in my bed in a void of solid black, eyes wide, gasping for air. My heart started to pound and I knew that if I didn't do something, I would die. I clenched my eyes shut and focused on myself. I pictured my body and put everything I had into trying to pull myself back to it. Then I opened them, and I was standing.

I was outside the building where I'd met the witches. It was pouring rain. I looked around me frantically. What was this? I raised my hands slowly to my face. Eight fingers on each. I was dreaming. I was asleep. A loud slam came from behind me and I whirled around to face the doors of the building, where it was now billowing out – the being from my room, the thick smoke in which it always appeared, was pouring out of the doors in a rush, and into the sky, creating a thick fog over everything. The entity's presence encompassed everything.

There was nowhere to run, and I did the only thing that I thought might help. Call it instinct, but I pressed my arms to my sides, squeezed my feet together, and tightened every muscle in my body. I stood there, frozen, condensing myself, and then fought with my mind. I clenched my eyes again, the way I had before, and focused my mind on the smoke, pictured a light pouring out of me, piercing the black sky it'd created. I opened my eyes and looked up, but nothing had changed. Panic rose in me, and the smoke began to solidify, gather, and then funnel towards the ground. It surrounded me like a twister and I was its centre. As it swirled around me, I dropped to the ground, balling myself up. I focused on the light again, trying to pierce it in any way I could. I opened my eyes, desperately hoping I was doing something to help, and I saw the blackness falling away from me. No, no -- it wasn't falling. It was me. I was falling, tumbling through a thick, black oblivion. There was nothing to hold on to and my limbs had flailed apart from each other. All I could do was fall.

I landed hard, and heard my own voice release a piercing scream that I wasn't quite aware of. I opened my eyes. I was back on my bed. The witches were standing before it. They nodded simply, then left the room. I jumped off my bed, desperate to know what happened, what they'd done, and ran to my bedroom door. They weren't in the hall. They were nowhere. Gone. I didn't know what exactly had happened, or if they'd even done me any good. I supposed I would have to wait until that night, and hope for the best.

Runner Up

Nathan S. M. Knapp

Nathan S.M. Knapp is a writer, teacher, and baseball fanatic. His short fiction has previously appeared in One Throne Magazine. He lives in Eastern Ontario.

You can follow Nathan on Twitter:

@WesternNate

The Monsters Outside the Well

NATHAN S. M. KNAPP

When I was twelve I lost my friend, Stevie. I say "lost" because that's what you're supposed to say in polite society. But I guess this isn't about being polite, is it? He died. Still too polite? Alright, he was killed. I'm not sure if it was murder or not, but he was definitely killed. No one ever found the body, but I know where it is. If there's anything left that is.

It started when my dad asked my friends and me to tear up a patch of earth in the backyard to make room for a new garden he was planting. The soil was too rocky for a rototiller. It had to be all done by hand. He bribed us with pizza for dinner if we agreed to do the work for him. How could we resist?

There were five of us altogether: myself, Kyle, Rob, Devin and Stevie. We all lived in a small town called Shawville. Looking back, it was a nice enough place to grow up, but as a twelve-year-old boy it sometimes felt maddeningly dull.

My dad put four stakes in the ground to show us the area to be excavated. The ground was covered with rye grass that had buried its roots in twisting lines. It gripped the earth like a rock-climber scaling a mountain, and we were the hand of God pulling it off the cliff face. I guess in a way that's exactly what we were doing.

Once we tore out the rye grass, our shovels started clanking against rock. We had no choice but to get down on our hands and knees and pull out the rocks one by one. It was painful work. It didn't take long before our backs were aching, our knuckles were scratched and bleeding, and the sun felt too hot for early May. But we kept going.

We were almost finished when our shovels hit a large stone buried in the earth. We struck it like synchronized drummers banging on a stone bass drum.

After exchanging glances, we started uncovering the rock by pulling out the dirt that had settled against it. But there was something underneath the rock. At first we thought it was sitting on top of more rocks, but then Devin extracted one from the ground. He held it up to the sun. It was an ancient red-clay brick. Mortar still clung to its side, like frosting on a forgotten cake.

We kept digging and found more bricks. We continued excavating and uncovered a round wall of red bricks. The large grey stone was sitting on top, like a lid. As we dug deeper the wall transitioned from brick to stone, all held in place with mortar. We uncovered it as best we could and then we all sat back on the grass, marvelling at what we'd found.

Devin was the first to say it. It came out in a hushed whisper, as if he were telling us something profane in church, "It's an old well."

Kyle whistled softly and said, "This is awesome. How old do you think it is?"

I shrugged my shoulders and said, "I dunno. Maybe a hundred years old. Maybe more."

Devin grinned and asked, "Anyone else want to see what it looks like inside?"

There was a cacophony of eager shouts. I like to think that I knew it was a bad idea at the time, but that would be lying. The only one who really protested was Stevie. He kept warning us about how dangerous it could be, but all he got for his caution was condescending insults from the rest of us. To shut him up we made him a deal. We promised that after we looked inside we would close it back up.

We got to work by backfilling one side of the pit beside the well with dirt, to make sure that we had a ledge to roll the capstone onto. Then we wedged our shovels and a pickaxe underneath the stone and started prying. It took several tries and all of our strength, but finally we managed to roll the stone off of the well. We all fell back from the final heaving effort and an instant later our faces were clustered over the vertical tunnel. We couldn't see anything. But the smell was overwhelming. It didn't smell bad, just foreign.

"Okay," Devin said, "let's see what's down there. Rob, go grab a flashlight or something from the house. Kyle, do you have any of your M-80s?"

Kyle grinned and nodded. "Yeah, they're in my backpack. I'll be right back."

Devin and I started dropping stones down the well. We could hear the stones hitting the bottom. Some of them made the sound of stone striking against stone; one made a shallow splashing noise; and the last one we dropped made a soft thudding noise, as if it landed against something more yielding than rock.

Kyle came back and was laying out the firecrackers on the grass, counting out how many he had and smoothing out the wicks. Rob returned with a Mag-Lite.

Stevie pleaded with us to stop. He warned us that the well might collapse if we dropped the firecrackers into it.

Kyle ignored him. He lit a firecracker and dropped it down. The firecracker hit the stone bottom of the well and exploded in a burst of fire and sound. We all howled with excitement and exchanged high-fives. All of us except Stevie. He was shouting something at us, but Devin had already lit the next firecracker and dropped it down the well. We all exploded into another celebration as the firecracker boomed from the bottom of the well.

Stevie kept shouting. Finally we heard him. "Guys, there's something down there! We gotta put the rock back."

We called him a pussy and Kyle handed out M-80s to all of us. We agreed to drop them simultaneously. Stevie kept looking into the well. He started shouting something about seeing eyes staring back at him. He moved to the far side of the rock and started pushing, but it wouldn't budge. We ignored him and let go of the firecrackers in one synchronized drop and the explosion was deafening. A small puff of dust came up out of the hole.

We shouted and hollered with excitement. Except for Stevie. He was grimacing with the effort of pushing the stone. Tears streaked down his dirty face.

He shrieked at us, "Guys, help. Push the stone back. There's something down there!"

Devin must have seen the terror in Stevie's face because he decided to peer down into the hole. He jumped back like he had been electrocuted. I figured Devin was putting us on, but I peeked my head over the hole just the same. Maybe it was just the shadows inside the well. Maybe it was a shared delusion, a testament to the power of suggestion. But whatever the case, I swear I saw some kind of shadow creature climbing the rock wall of the well.

Devin screamed this time, "Guys, there's actually something down there! We gotta get the stone back on top."

"Good one Devin," Kyle laughed.

But then he looked into the hole and he too must have seen the monster coming up the wall because he jumped back in terror.

We all joined Stevie in pushing the stone back. It wasn't moving though. In our fear we forgot how we moved it in the first place, by using the pickaxe and our shovels as levers. Maybe if we remembered things would have ended differently.

Out of desperation Stevie jumped into the pit. He wrapped his arms around the rock, pulling it towards him. It was a good way to leverage the rock, but it also meant that his body was exposed, leaning across the opening of the well. It was a crazy move. Despite all of our insults about Stevie being a coward, he was the only one brave enough to expose his body like that.

Just when I thought the stone would never move, it finally settled itself halfway across the opening, leaving a gap nearly two feet wide. We kept pushing but it refused to move any further.

"Come on guys, just anoth–" Stevie didn't get a chance to finish.

His head snapped forward, bashing against the capstone, leaving a sheet of crimson stain, and then his body was yanked into the hole in a demented corkscrew motion. We screamed, but it still didn't drown out the horrible echoing of Stevie's body hitting the bottom of the well. We kept screaming, but somehow we still heard the monster snapping its shadowed jaws up and down. The sound was punctuated with the horrible cracking sound of Stevie's bones splintering.

Eventually we stopped screaming. There was silence from the well and then we heard scraping sounds. We recognized the sound this time. The shadow creature was climbing up the wall to snatch another one of us.

We pushed against the stone with desperation. God knows why, but the rock moved easier than before and it settled itself back into position. We all waited for the beast to knock the stone off of the well opening, but nothing happened. It didn't even shudder.

We buried it as much as we could, tears streaking our dirty faces, but no one said anything. There was a search for Stevie, but of course he was never found. You couldn't even see the well or the capstone anymore. We filled in the hole we tore up with dozens of bags of black earth and my dad planted tomato plants that evening.

The police investigated Stevie's disappearance and they questioned all of us separately. We all told the same story: Stevie helped us clear the garden and then he walked home alone. We didn't know what happened to him after that. We knew that telling anyone the truth would mean the capstone would come off again. If the monster could live down there for a hundred years and still be alive, then it could probably live down there forever, waiting for someone else to open its door.

It's funny how life finds a way to repeat itself, if you wait long enough. It revolves like an orbit, bringing you back to the same place you were years before. I'm a father now and I have a son. He's twelve. I live in the same house. My dad left it to me when he died. I plant vegetables every spring – sometimes even tomatoes – in that same patch of ground. I try not to think of Stevie at the bottom of the well, but lately the memory of it returns with increasing frequency. Except the memory has changed over the years. And now I'm not sure which version is the truth and which one's a fantasy.

I used to think that we all saw the shadow creature climbing the wall of the well, but I'm not so sure anymore. I know that Stevie saw it, or at least his mind insisted that it was there. But like anyone who's ever been alone at night in a dark house, it's very easy to see or hear things that aren't really there. The creature was so real for Stevie that maybe he convinced the rest of us that it was there. Even if it wasn't.

Because in my dreams, I see the event unfolding a different way. This time there is no creature that pulls Stevie into the black hole of the well. Instead it was me. I snuck up behind him and pushed him. I'm not sure if I was trying to scare him or hurt him, or worse… But I do know that my dream self enjoyed the pushing. And it wasn't just my hands on Stevie's back. Devin pushed too. And so did Rob and Kyle. We all pushed him and his head struck the capstone, smearing it crimson, and we shoved his body inside, twisting it as needed to make it fit. And then it dropped to the cold bottom. We rolled the capstone back without saying a word and in my dream… we were smiling. There was no monster inside the well. Only four monsters outside of it.

We buried the well and misled the police, but I'm not sure why. Maybe we were scared of a monster deep below, or maybe we were covering up the murder of our friend. And if that's true, how can it be that we've gone on to live normal lives, without guilt or regret?

For the life of me, I don't know what happened that day. Maybe we all wanted to hurt Stevie for being such a coward. Or we were just trying to scare him, but it went too far. Maybe something really was buried in that old well, but that doesn't mean it was a monster. It could have been some kind of toxin that causes homicidal behaviour, or a demon floated out and lodged itself in our minds just long enough to get us to murder our friend. I don't really know. The only thing I'm sure of is that as each day passes, I become less and less sure that there really was a shadow creature in the well. It does sound childish, doesn't it? The kind of story you tell around a campfire. Scary enough for adolescents, but nothing dark enough to terrify an adult.

Because adults know that there is a shadow creature living inside each of us. It's there, buried beneath the ground, at the bottom of a forgotten well at the back of the mind, sealed with a capstone. And I'll bet if you really listen, you can hear your own shadow creature crawling up the inside of the wall. Because you have one, just as surely as I do. The danger is once you let it out, it's very difficult to bury it again. Somehow my friends and I were able to that day, but I can almost feel the capstone shuddering with my shadow creature's efforts to lift it off.

I know there's only one way to find out what really happened. If the creature is real, then it will still surely be waiting for someone to lift the capstone from its dungeon. And I'll see it climbing up to pull me down. But if it's not real – if it never really existed – then I'll find the adolescent bones of my friend Stevie piled at the bottom of the well. And I'll know that I pushed him that day.

I've resolved myself to find out what happened. I'm going to pull off the capstone again. I know I can't do it alone. It's okay, though. My son will be there to help. I've never told him, but he sort of reminds me of my friend Stevie.

Fourth Place Winner (Tie)

Dennis Stein

Dennis Stein lives in Brockville, Ontario, not far from the scenic Thousand Islands. He enjoys writing in a wide variety of genres, and regularly writes historical and human interest articles for several local publications. He is also the author of the Young Adult Fantasy series "The Gecko's Gate". Most of his writing is done on an old iPod Touch, which he carries with him wherever he goes.

The Lantern

DENNIS STEIN

"You can have the lantern for free," said the strange, grey-haired old shop keeper without looking up from his newspaper. "Just remember, once you take it, you can't un-take it."

He was now looking directly at me, a soft grin on his ancient face. I supposed it was his idea of a joke, meaning "no returns or refunds." His eyes seemed to look through me as the words left his mouth. But he was offering it to me for free, surprisingly enough, so the whole thing made no sense. I adjusted my purse in what I knew was a nervous response, and tucked my short blonde hair behind an ear, pulling my fall jacket tighter around me. He seemed not to notice, and I tried to relax, realizing that this old man wasn't concerned with how I looked, or who I was.

The lantern in question looked like it was from the early 1800s, or even before, but it stood there on the counter clean and perfect, its black metal and clear glass making it look as if it were made only yesterday. The hand blown glass was something that could not be found in this modern age. The imperfections of bubbles and warps in its clear surface caught the late afternoon sun streaming through the dusty windows.

Something about it drew me in, and I couldn't remove my eyes from it. It held my gaze, its oil burning wick clean and bright, ready to light my way. I had to have it… I thanked him very politely, lifting it up gently off of the counter by its wire handle, and turned to leave. I wasn't more than a few steps from the front door, when the old man broke the silence in the antique shop one last time.

"Some things in this world are better off not being illuminated...," he said quietly.

I looked back at him one last time as I reached for the door handle, but he never looked up from his newspaper.

A bell clanged noisily against the glass door as I left the shop, announcing my departure from the shop as I emerged into the late afternoon sun which nearly blinded me with its warm radiance. I hadn't even meant to go in there, but the curiosities that met my eyes as I walked past on my way out of the bank simply could not be ignored. I looked at my watch quickly, registering the hour as I cursed softly at myself for taking too much time. I had to be available tonight for a conference call, even though I was finished at the office for the day. I had to haul ass.

Cradling the lantern in the crook of my arm, I fumbled with the door of the car, practically falling into the driver's seat in my haste. I set my new acquisition carefully in the passenger's seat and headed off. The sun was already sinking below the horizon as I sped across town, drawing the visor down against the glare of the sun's last rays. I wanted to get it home, into a comfy spot where it would be a conversation piece in the old house in which I lived. It would fit perfectly. There was a lot of history in my old home, dating back to the settlement of the area. Perhaps it would be the finishing touch to complete the space. I didn't care either way-- it was cool.

Darkness had fallen as I pulled up the driveway to the house. I reached back and grabbed my briefcase from the back seat and carefully lifted the lantern from its perch in the seat beside me. Getting back to the house was my favourite part of the day. It was my sanctuary, a utopian solace away from the busy life of the city. I had not yet married, although I'd had a few relationships that had failed, but I preferred my life the way it was anyway. I was far too busy to entertain another person in my life right now. I didn't feel the need to share my time, or my life with someone else who might turn out to be NOT like me.

I inserted my key and opened the door and was greeted immediately by the only other life form which I shared my space with: the cat. He rubbed up against my legs in the shadows of the front entrance as I shut the door behind me, meowing at me to follow him to the kitchen to fetch his food for him. Such was our routine. I turned on some lights as I made my way along behind him, illuminating the house against its darkness, and tossed my purse and jacket aside on the couch. I carried the lantern carefully into the kitchen and placed it on the counter before indulging the cat's request.

Two hours later, all was well. I switched off the speaker phone ending my conference call at the kitchen island as the cat lay next to the phone, purring in satisfaction. It was finally the end of another day. But my eyes were drawn back to the lantern, sitting close by, as I had not decided where I would display it.

I fumbled around in one of the drawers of the island. I found an old lighter, a remnant of when I used to smoke. I gently lifted the glass in its housing, and held the flame to the wick. It lit quickly, surprising me. Its glow filled the kitchen. The cat immediately looked toward the bright flame from the lantern, and sat up from his comfy post beside the phone. His wide green eyes watched the flickering flame for only a moment, before he drew back, hissing at it. Quickly jumping off of the island, he headed off towards the back of the house. I raised an eyebrow at his sudden departure.

Despite my surprise at the cat's reaction, my gaze was drawn back to the flickering fire inside the lantern's glass. It was bright, but the rest of the kitchen seemed to darken into shadow with its light, as if the lantern were the only light in the room. A sudden movement caught the corner of my eye, distracting me momentarily. But as I surveyed the kitchen, nothing seemed amiss. I dismissed the thought, assuming that my fatigued eyes and mind were playing tricks on me. Leaning forward, I blew out the flame and lowered the glass back into place. It was time to retire for the night.

The cat apprehensively reappeared and followed me up the stairs to bed. But he didn't cuddle up alongside my legs like he normally would, but instead remained alert near the bottom of the bed as I slid into unconsciousness, the occasional flick of his tail against the bed frame a quiet reminder of his presence. I sank into the thick comforter, happy and warm with my sentinel watching over me. A song that I had heard on the radio played over and over in my head as I succumbed to sleep, and I embraced the dark warmth of the night.

My eyes shot open in the darkness, and I realized slowly that it was still the early hours of the morning. I rolled over quickly, looking at the digital alarm clock on the night stand. The red illuminated numbers that should have been there were absent. Great--the power was out. I fumbled around in the black, trying to get my bearings. Struggling out of bed, I somehow managed to find my housecoat, and slipped it on to cover up my nightgown in the dark, coming out of grogginess into the idea that it was irrelevant. I made my way out into the hall and down the stairs slowly, feeling my way along the cool painted surfaces of the walls. Once my hand fell on the light switch at the bottom of the steps, I absently tried flicking it back and forth to no avail.

I continued to fumble along in the pitch blackness until my hands finally brushed the kitchen island. Carefully I moved my hands along its surface, searching blindly for what I knew would light up the room. And there it was -- the lantern. My fingers landed gently on its cold polished steel, and I felt for the cigarette lighter that I had fortunately left immediately beside it.

It took a moment, but after a few flicks the wick lit up brilliantly, casting its light around me in the solid darkness of the kitchen. Its brilliance was strange somehow, not like the warm glow of an ordinary fire, but cold… almost artificial. I couldn't tear my eyes away from its mesmerizing glow.

I felt my heart skip a beat momentarily as I caught movement out of the corner of my vision. I turned slowly, my breath freezing in my throat as I lifted the lantern to light the dining room beside the kitchen. I fought to control my mind's instant panic as I grabbed the island with my other hand to keep my knees from buckling beneath me. There was a man sitting at my dining room table. I squinted through the darkness, every nerve in my body now on fire, and tried to make sense of the horror before me.

The man was black and his thin arms rested on the dark mahogany of my dining room table. It was difficult to discern his age, but to my eyes he looked to be in his fifties, but with very pale skin for someone who seemed to be of African descent. An old shotgun rested on the table beside him. His clothing was plain and looked fairly old. And there was blood. A lot of it. It pooled on the table and was spattered on the wall behind him. I forced myself to continue to breathe. His eyes never met mine, as though he was thinking about something distant, like he was unaware of my very presence. He turned his head suddenly, and I felt my stomach lurch. Half of his head was missing – his skull had been shattered and his blood-smeared brain looked like a ghoulish mess. I gasped abruptly when I saw this, but I was far too scared to worry about passing out. Then there was a noise, high and shrill. My mind fought to understand where it was coming from. It was me… I was screaming!

I grabbed the lantern, turned and ran, blindly, trying to get away from this horrible scene in which I was trapped. I reached the bottom of the stairs and flailed my way upward. My lungs were already on fire, and I gripped the swaying lantern, lighting my retreat up to the landing. Three steps further and I was inside my bedroom, slamming the door behind me and twisting the lock. It slid tightly with a metallic click that told me I might be safe, and I stopped for a moment, sucking in oxygen and trying to calm my heartbeat. I had a phone next to the bed, I could call 911. I would be safe.

I cursed softly, my brain registering the power outage, and the fact that my cordless phone would be useless. The swaying of the lantern slowed and the light it cast danced on the wall by beside the locked door. I leaned to rest my forehead against the wall for just a moment and thought reassuringly to myself that whatever was happening, it would all be okay. There was a slight creaking, both above and behind me. My breathing stopped again. I slowly raised my head off of the wall, and craned my neck to look in the direction of the sound. It was still very dark, despite the lantern's eerie glow, but I could sense movement in the room. I raised the lantern, hitching in breath as I saw this terrible thing swinging from the exposed old rafters of my bedroom.

It was a boy, probably in his late teens, hanging from a homemade noose, his face deathly white as he swung gently above my bed. The creaking was from the old rope chaffing against the wood. The boy's eyes were glazed, but he seemed to still be conscious. His shoe laces were untied on his simple leather shoes that crazily swung along with him. He raised his hand in silence, reaching out toward me in the gloom. He never looked at me, but his twitching body sent me fumbling for the door lock. I didn't scream -- I simply wanted out!

I opened the lock and twisted the doorknob, lunging out the door as soon as I could fit through. I had to get out of the house. I hurried down the stairway taking the steps two at a time while the lantern swung carelessly in my hand.

Reaching the kitchen, I told myself to ignore the dining room as I sprinted up the hallway toward the living room and the front door. I could see the cat ahead of me, already meowing impatiently, pawing at the door. His eyes were wide in his own fear.

The lantern's crazy swaying light lit the gloom of the living room as I sped through, and I stopped dead in my tracks, unable to go forward. There, ina rocking chair in front of me, was an old woman rocking slowly back and forth. Breathing heavily, I raised the lantern. Gooseflesh rose on my arms.

The old woman's hair was snow white and her skin was translucent. She stared at the floor in front of her as she rocked, her flowered dress covered in the crimson stain of blood. Drops of red fell from the rocking chair and gathered on the hardwood floor beneath her. My eyes grew wider as she raised her head to turn her face towards me. Her throat had been sliced from one side to the other, showing ancient tendons and sliced blood vessels. Another scream escaped me, long and loud. The smell of blood flooded my senses, its coppery liquid tang seemed to invade my mouth as I fought to breathe, fought to keep away from the border of insanity.

The floor lamp in the living room suddenly lit up and changed the horrifying scene before my eyes. The old woman was still there, still rocking, but she was transparent, as if only half there. I shook my head, trying to clear my vision, and wondering what kind of terrible dream I was trapped in. The floor lamp was one I always left on at night. The power was back on. I looked slowly back at the lantern and its strange flickering flame. Raising the glass, I blew it out, cursing softly at the burn I received from its surface.

The living room looked as it always did when I came home. The woman in the rocking chair was gone. The blood was gone. The bright light from the floor lamp lit up my perfect living area, nothing more. My heart started to slow down again.

"Some things in this world are better off not being illuminated..."

I looked back at the lantern with my eyes still wide in terror. Its polished black steel, and hand-blown glass were untarnished, its wick almost begging to be lit again. I took two steps to reach the heavy wood of the front door. Opening the entry with a loud creak, I threw the lantern out into the darkness, and heard its glass shatter on the walkway.

I stalked through the house and turned on every light. Reality returned, with every click of a light switch. The dining room and kitchen were fine, and showed no evidence of blood, nor any of the horrors I'd witnessed earlier.

I climbed the stairs to my bedroom. It was back to normal. My heartrate settled. Whatever had happened, it was over. But it had not been a dream.

I sank down onto the floor, putting my head in my hands. I could feel the cold sweat on my forehead. It took me several minutes to recover, and I struggled to my feet again and cast another quick glance around the room to re-affirm that everything was as it should be. The red numbers on the alarm clock flashed at me.

The lantern was gone, and would never show me those horrors again. I breathed in and out deeply then slowly headed out the door toward the stairs again. It seemed senseless to even think about going back to sleep.

My legs heavy, I made my way back down the stairs, holding the railing firmly. It seemed like it took forever to reach the bottom again, but finally my bare feet met the cool tiles of the kitchen floor. I raised my head, looking at the fully-lit kitchen. My heart stopped. It wasn't possible. The chill in my blood instantly returned, pounding in my ears as I choked in air.

The lantern sat on the island, its polished surface and bright glass reflecting the lights in the kitchen. It was here. How? I had heard it smash on the sidewalk outside…

"Just remember, once you take it, you can't un-take it."

Runner Up

Rod Martinez

Rod was born and raised in Tampa, Florida and was attracted to words at an early age. His first book "The Boy Who Liked To Read" was created in grade school. Eventually he discovered comic books, but his High School English teacher told him to try short story writing. He wrote middle grade adventure "The Juniors" that was picked up by a publisher, and the rest – as they say, is history.

You can find Rod at his website:
http://rodmartinez.us

Bella's Place

ROD MARTINEZ

She was surrounded by steel, glass and concrete, but Bella preferred it this way. This was home. After a long day at work she could finally settle in, relax, no one to watch her, no one to gaze her way and do a double take. Because she was used to this, all day long at work, getting strange looks from people all around her. Was it her golden curly locks or the free flowing dress she liked to wear? It was something she pondered a lot, but this was not a time to worry about it. No, Bella was home, and she was fine being home, even now at this late hour of 10 p.m.

The metropolis she called home was Tampa, Florida and she was no stranger to the night life, though she never went out. No, Ybor City, SOHO, Channelside – not even the soothing waters under the Gandy Bridge would be graced by her presence. She was home and this was paradise. But Bella had one vice, though she didn't consider it one -- Bella loved to read. To some, reading was boring; to others it was a pleasure, a sideline after or during a quick break or even a way to spend leisure time. To Bella it was a voracious appetite that needed quenching, nightly. It was all she did at night till the wee hours of the morning when she had to get back up for work.

Her furniture was covered in books -- a shelf here, a stand there -- but there was no one to complain about it; this was Bella's place. She read by a schedule she placed on herself and this was the beginning of Florida Classics week for her so she was ready to dig into Marjorie Kinnan Rawlings tonight. Bella lived alone, in a home designed like no other in all of Tampa. She was lucky, and she knew it. And though outside others dealt with the warm Florida climate, she sat in cool comfort in her favorite chair with her copy of The Yearling in her grasp. She smiled as she stared out through the huge side window into a dark cityscape.

Night brought a new life to Tampa with bustling clubs, bars and restaurants and yes, even the famous strip clubs for which the city was known. But Bella would have none of it -- she was content being alone at home, alone in Bella's place.

Solitude was normal to her, no family, no pets – just her and her books -- and she liked that. Sure it might sound selfish, but this was all she knew.

There was a move to turn Downtown Tampa into a residential haven and it was a challenge for many a developer – but the condos lined up and down the one way streets making it easy targets for the young professionals in the area. Bella would see neighbors walking their dogs up and down the streets through the window. but never chose to engage them. No, Bella adored her solitude – being surrounded by people made her stiffen up, she didn't like that feeling. She was content, alone, in Bella's place. She sat back, cracked open the book – and sighed in a smile.

CLINK!

The metallic sound had made her jump. She was alone-- she knew she was alone-- so why did something make a noise? Noises from the outside were a common thing, but this sound came from within her home, and not too far from where she sat.

"Hello?" she called. It was actually almost a whisper, she didn't want to be afraid, but she wasn't expecting company and this intrusion wasn't expected.

THONK!

Another noise. She put the book down. That was clearly a sound pretty close to where she sat and almost sounded like something had fallen off of a shelf. She started to fret. What if someone had broken in? She reached for the closest thing she might use as a weapon. There wasn't much around her, but there – she found it, an artist's paint brush. It was sitting next to her on the Corian surfaced desk.

"Hello? I can hear you. I… I have a weapon," she said, mustering her best brave face.

Whoever or whatever it was didn't acknowledge or even offer a noise.

"The nerve," she thought to herself. "Why do people break into other people's homes?" She was a good distance from the phone; there was no way she'd make it there if the person jumped out at her. She'd wait it out; he had to make another move. This time she reached over, looking for anything else she might use in case of defense. She felt on the counter, something round, heavy – it felt like the metallic time piece a maintenance man had left after trying to fix her clock. She cupped her fingers around it and held it to her side.

The silence, for the first time in her huge home – was unnerving. She looked out the huge picture window, so many cars driving by… if only one of them would stop, stop and see what was going on inside. Stop to help her.

Bella stood at the ready, half frightened out of her wits, and half curious. But no other sound occurred. She would not sleep tonight, she felt that if she moved – then whoever this intruder was would follow her. She was ready to defend herself, but she didn't really want to entice a fight. No, she would hold her ground, she would stand at the ready – and she knew where to stand.

There was a pedestal not far from where she was crouched. It was in the shadows, just a couple of feet away. They wouldn't see her there, and once they did – she'd be in a position to do something. She could jump the person and use the clock piece she'd found, or maybe even the paint brush – if needed. Bella would not move once she got on the stand, she would stay right where she was, even if it took all night… and wait.

*****

Daylight. Tuesday morning and it was as usual as any other day. The Westshore area filled with cars coming over the bridge from Pinellas for those that worked in Hillsborough. South Tampa swelled with school buses and parents rushing the kids to school. Scenic Bayshore Boulevard -- with its world's longest sidewalk -- proved again to be the best pedestrian and bike trafficking spot in the area. New Tampa and Brandon area's roads were at their usual, slow and annoying. Downtown Tampa bustled in normal fashion with traffic -- people coming in to work, tourists enjoying the sights and vendors readying for another busy day. The famous minarets of the University of Tampa covered the background like a beautifully painted canvas as the sun rose over the east skyscraper panorama.

Just outside the Courthouse a man held a wooden cross and smiled as jurors, attorneys and the public slowly entered through the security gates. Over at the Tampa-Hillsborough Public Library's main building, the doors opened and customers rushed in, some to get the morning paper, some for the book they had put on reserve, many to use the computers that were lined up in the first and second floor areas.

A mother holding her young child by the hand headed straight for the reference desk while fumbling with her iPhone.

"Hi, I need to find a book for my son on the Spanish American War?"

"Sure ma'am," the librarian smiled, "… those books would be right in that area. Follow me and I'll show you."

She pointed just behind the mother who acted to move, but was then suddenly stopped by her son who was yanking hardly on her right hand.

"Mommy?"

"Yes, David?"

"That statue, she winked at me!" His eyebrows curled down in a confused curiosity.

"What did you say, dear?"

He pointed up.

"Her, the statue with the gold curly hair and holding a paintbrush in her hand and that clock thing… She winked at me."

The busy mother turned, taking in the sight of the magnificent bronze statue.

"Ahhh," the librarian smiled walking over to the child. "… That is Bella, Bella Apollonia. She is the Art Muse. She does seem to possess some sort of life, doesn't she?"

"But… she winked at me."

"She did? Well, she loves children you know… children and books." The librarian smiled.

"Come, David. We have to find your book," the mother rushed.

They walked away into the stacks.

"Hey, uh, Lori?" called a fellow co-worker.

The librarian turned.

"Yes?"

"We had all the books put away last night, but this copy of The Yearling was sitting on that chair next to the window. Did you pull it for a customer?"

"No, Tim, we just opened and I just sat down here when these customers approached."

"Oh, hmm, weird, huh?"

"Yeah, maybe Bella here wanted to get in some last minute reading in the middle of the night." She pointed back at the statue and chuckled.

"Ha, yeah – right."

He walked away with a smirk on his face. Then passing the catalog computer he saw a metal book end on the floor, bent down and picked it up. No sooner had he stood up to replace it when it slipped out of his hand and dropped to the floor again.

CLANK!

"Geez!"

He scooped it up and placed it back on the top shelf of reference books, as he glanced back at Bella. He could have sworn that he'd seen the statue flinch at the sound of the metal book end hitting the floor when he'd dropped it. He stopped, turned around fully and stared closely at the bronze piece of art, then rubbed his chin.

"Na…" Then he walked away.

Bella smiled.

THE END

*Note, Bella is actually a real statue sitting on the public floor of the Tampa-Hillsborough Public Library in Downtown Tampa, Florida – USA

Runner Up
J.P. Frost

J.P. Frost was raised in Ontario's beautiful Almaguin Highlands. He has lived in the Middle East and spent extended time in West Africa and Northern Europe. He is currently a graduate student at McMaster University in Hamilton.

Tana mu xi

J.P. FROST

Looking back on it, I realize now that I moved to Africa to get away from the old ghosts in my life, the friends who had slowly distanced themselves from me, the family members who'd never called or even sent an email, the failed relationships. I had no idea then that the place I thought of as a refuge would end up introducing me to new ghosts, ghosts that continue to haunt my dreams and fuel a powerful fear of sleep that medications, meditation, and all the warm milk in the world can't fix. Let me tell you what happened.

When I landed in Conakry things were pretty different. First of all, I was soon surrounded by a crowd of children begging for money. These kids had missing limbs, scabs and dust all over them. One little guy even had a big ball of scar tissue bulging off his face. They wanted to shake my hand, but I was freaked out, thinking I might catch something from them. In the end, the Canadian in me won out and I ended up shaking a few of their hands, feeling the crusted scabs scraping against my smooth palm. A man who was walking beside me told me to ignore them. He was dressed in shorts and a white collared shirt, open at the top. He moved with the ease of someone who had been in these kinds of airports before. But I didn't know if I could ignore these kids, in fact, I was pretty horrified by the shape they seemed to be in.

"If you help one," he said, "they'll all want help. Besides, by encouraging them you only make it harder the next time we all come through here."

Trying not to think about fate and why I was born in the place I was, and why these kids were born where they were, I tightened my grip on my bag and pressed through the crowd, making a mental note to find the small bottle of hand sanitizer packed in my luggage. If this was going to be a common experience in Guinea, I wasn't sure if I had made the right choice to come here.

I would see that guy in the white shirt again. The next time we met though, he wouldn't be keeping it together so well. By that time, I had moved farther into the country, closer to the forest region. People told me diamond smugglers would cross through there from Sierra Leone. I never saw any smugglers, or diamonds, but I wouldn't be surprised if people used the forest to move undetected through the country.

It was a maze of dark trails and paths so narrow only one person could walk down them at a time. The trees were truly massive, rivaling or even surpassing many of the trees I grew up playing in or under in Northern Ontario. Every now and then you'd come across a really massive one, its roots sitting up on top of the soil like giant coiled snakes, as thick as a person. You could walk along these roots towards the tree, like a kind of elevated boardwalk, until they joined the tree and curved into the shape of thick rocket fins, supporting the base. Up close you could see the wicked looking thorns sticking out all over the trunk, dashing any of the fantasies you had about how cool it would be to climb it.

One day I was with a friend and I remarked casually to him that a particular tree we were looking at had enough wood in it to make a house for a whole family. He looked like someone had told him that his mother died. His eyes widened, nostrils flared, and his mouth hung open like he was going to cry.

"No, no, no, no, no," he said, his voice sounding the way his face looked. "This is a sacred tree. We can never cut it down."

A sacred tree?

"What makes it a sacred tree?" I asked him.

Apparently, when the founding family of a village stakes out some land to settle on, the uncle of the family digs a hole as deep as a man, takes his virgin niece and stands her up in it, then puts a bowl on her head. He places a seed in the bowl, a seed from one of these giant sacred trees, and then he buries her alive. The tree that grows up out of the girl's dead body becomes a sacred tree. People offer food sacrifices to it and cut the throats of chickens at the base. Needless to say I couldn't look at those trees the same way again. One minute I was admiring it for its lumber producing potential. The next I felt as if a dark shadow had been pulled over me. I started to get goose bumps whenever I looked at it, that big bloodsucking tree. But it was the same tree. Nothing had changed but my perspective.

As you can imagine, I started to realize that there were a lot of things I didn't know about my new home. By the time I met the guy from the airport again, a month had gone by. A month in Africa doesn't mean anything. You may as well snap your fingers and call it a month. In that time, I had crossed the country and made it into the southern forested regions where they said there were cannibal cults. A Christian missionary family, trying to save souls for Jesus told me that this wasn't true and that it was just rumour. But an old Jehovah's Witness missionary living in the middle of nowhere told me that he thought it was true. The few Peace Corps workers I met hadn't heard of anything, but then again, they didn't look like they got out much. The locals wouldn't tell me a damn thing. The closer people lived to the missionaries, the more likely they were to keep secrets or outright lie to you. I'm pretty sure there was an inverse relationship between the two. Eventually I made up my mind that the cannibal rumour couldn't be true. I mean, cannibals? Come on! It made me laugh to think I ever took it seriously. That old JW was probably nuts before he even got to Guinea. He had to be. He was a JW.

That's what I told myself anyway. As it turns out there were cannibal cults in Guinea, at least one anyway. I was following a friend down one of those dark forest paths when all of a sudden we were surrounded by guys with machine guns. Now I've stared down the barrel of a gun before, once in Jordan at a security checkpoint, and once during a pellet gun war at a friend's house. If these guys wanted us dead, we'd be dead already. They were probably going to rob us, which meant they'd take my passport, phone, cash, and beat us up a bit.

That's when my friend thought he'd try to run. His actions put me in a pickle. If I ran, I'd probably get shot. If I stood still they'd probably shoot me anyway in the excitement, thinking I was going to run, too. The funny thing was, they didn't shoot my friend, but started to chase him, which didn't make sense because obviously a bullet could travel a lot faster. That's when I remembered hearing back in Conakry that lots of guys in the forest have guns but can't afford bullets for them. If these guys had bullets they probably would have blasted my friend. Right then and there I decided to make a run for it. Unfortunately, in the time I had been thinking, one of the robbers had snuck up from behind and clubbed me with something over the head. I woke up with a throbbing headache and tied to a chair.

That's when I saw my airport friend. He was sitting next to the guy who had tried to make a run for it in the forest, and obviously didn't make it. They were in rough shape. Both of them had their arms tied behind their backs and a stick was tied behind their knees, holding them up in an uncomfortable position. Dried blood was crusted on airport guy's neck where it had run down from the top of his head. Guess they'd whacked him, too. One of the men standing across from me noticed that I was awake and smiled at me.

"Tana mu xi?" he asked. This was a local greeting, kind of like "how's it going?" only under these circumstances it was ironic because the words meant, "is there evil in your day?"

Damn right there's evil in my day! I replied with the traditional greeting that sounds like I'm wondering out loud about something, "uhhhHH," but really just means "no, there is no evil."

By this time, I was starting to get pretty worried. What were these guys going to do to us? I didn't have to wait long to find out. Out of the corner of my eye I noticed some movement. A small figure shuffled over to me and stuck out its hand. It was one of the children from the airport, the one with a ball of scar tissue on his face. I bent my wrist to stick my hand out to him, the ropes holding the rest of my arm tightly. Again I felt the scabby hand take mine. He smiled. He said something I couldn't understand and then shuffled over to the other two men who were tied up. Rather than stick his hand out to them, he started to yell.

My friend, who could speak the language, started crying, and the white-shirted man didn't blink. If he knew what was going on, he certainly didn't reveal it.

The boy shouted someone's name: "Dansa!" and moved away from the other men. A big guy, presumably Dansa, walked up to them and pulled out a knife. It must have had a ten-inch blade on it. He approached my crying friend and laid the sharp edge against his throat, now bulging with veins as he cried and tried to pull away. Curling his fingers into my friend's hair, he slowly pulled the blade under the jaw line from one side to the other. For a split second before the blood came out you could see the flesh pull apart like someone was cutting open the soft belly of a fish. Instead of fish guts though, there was blood -- waves and tides of blood pouring out. My friend's cries became gurgles, and then a rush of air and blood, like water coming out of a garden hose that you haven't use for a while.

I closed my eyes and turned my head. I didn't know him that well, but Jesus Christ, he was a decent guy.

By now, white shirt guy must have caught on to what was happening and started yelling at me. "Tell them to fucking stop!" Like I could do anything.

I moaned, "No, no, no, no," but no one paid any attention to me. By then I had opened my eyes again and watched Dansa untie my friend's arms and let his body dangle forward, the blood draining out of his neck and on to the ground. His head had twisted off to one side and was just dangling from the neck vertebrae. It didn't look real, I thought. Jesus, I needed it not to look real.

White shirt man was really freaking out. His face was purple and he swore at the big man moving closer to him. "Untie me, you motherfucker!" he was screaming. Some of the men watching started to laugh and called out to Dansa, probably asking him if he was going to let airport guy talk to him like that.

Dansa's answer came in the form of a knife sticking sideways through white shirt guy's throat. The back of the blade rested against the front of the spinal column while the knifepoint stuck out the other side of his neck. In one move Dansa pulled the knife forward and opened up the front of his victim's throat.

I didn't look away that time. Maybe I should have.

What followed next was a blur. The bodies were bled dry, were stripped of clothing and then butchered. I was made to sit down on a plastic mat near the fire. I was still tied up, but at least my legs were free. There I watched as they cooked the arms and legs of my colleagues over the flames, the fat popping and hissing through the fissured skin.

After a while the boy came back to me carrying a piece of meat. He held it out, encouraging me to eat it. I knew what it was. I didn't dare refuse him though, opting to just play along with whatever they were doing. I took a bite and he smiled. He took a bite too. It didn't taste that bad actually.

I won't bore you with the details of my departure from the forest region. The cult let me go once I ate with them. I suppose they knew that if I reported them I'd also be implicated in the cannibalism.

So now, since moving back to Canada I've had the strange feeling of craving that meat again. I feel torn between knowing it's wrong, and wanting to taste the delicious flesh in my mouth. This is going to sound weird, but people have taken on another quality when I look at them. It's a quality they never had before: I wonder what they'd taste like. I've been pretty good about suppressing that curiosity, in fact, I've only given into it once or twice.

If you're ever travelling through and would like to hear a great story, I'd be thrilled if you stopped by for conversation and a meal. It's amazing what a change of perspective will do.

Runner Up
Rick Weiss

Rick Weiss is a communication professional living in Toronto, Ontario, Canada, and a long time fan of fantasy and science fiction. Through his career, Rick has shared stories about corporate achievements. In 2015, Rick began writing sci-fi, branching out into imaginative storytelling.

You can find Rick online at:
http://rickweiss.ca
Twitter: @RickWeiss

Have You Dreamt of Dragons

RICK WEISS

When you fall asleep in your own bedroom, beside your better half, you implicitly expect to awake in the same place.

I went to sleep on a regular Tuesday night at my regular time. Cheryl and I had sex. We passed out immediately. Our two kids – 4 and 7 years old – were sound asleep in their bunks in the second bedroom of our high-rise apartment.

My next memory is feeling cold metal on my naked back as I groggily regained consciousness.

Raising my hands up to help rub my eyes open with a yawn, another odd sensation struck me. Like when you fall asleep on your arm and you wake up unable to move it. Neither of my arms would move. I was paralyzed.

Squinting in the darkness, I had no control over my body, no idea where I was. I tried to call out to my wife.

"CHERYL!"

Her name rang loudly through my mind, echoing inside my head. My voice did not strike my eardrums.

My eyes could swivel. I could control my eyes. Not that it did much when my eyelids could hardly open. They couldn't close either.

"WHERE AM I?"

Glancing around the room, I couldn't see much. The little light there was radiated from strange displays mounted to structures around the room. They were much darker than the computer screens we're accustomed to.

It reminded me of the time I toured a submarine at the local summer exhibition. The air was stale and metallic. A hum of unknown systems gently vibrated the table beneath my spine. Other sounds arose through the ambient drone; pings, clanks.

Am I on a submarine? I thought. It didn't make any sense.

At least I know I can hear. My ears work. I took some minor solace in that.

This is ridiculous. A nightmare. That's it; it has to be a dream. There's no other possible explanation, I thought to myself.

I shifted my eyes to my left and saw a human arm that was enclosed in a transparent cylinder connected to an odd machine.

Is that MY arm? Why would I even think that? Still, I couldn't put the thought to rest. The thought drilled into my conscious psyche.

No way. It's not mine. My arm is where it's always been – attached to my shoulder! I tried to reassure myself.

Are you really sure? Was my subconscious response.

Of course, I couldn't be sure. The simple action of looking at my left arm, or reaching for it with my right arm escaped me.

An electrical crackle came from the machine holding the arm-cylinder-thing. The arm flinched. I swear I felt the spark rush up my spine. My only other feeling was the metal beneath my back and the chill. The sensation was like waiting in a paper gown in my doctor's office. Five minutes of waiting feels like an eternity when your skin is covered in goose bumps.

Another crackle sounded. The arm flinched. Another jolt raced up my spine.

Oh, God. I'm losing it. This is a nightmare and I will wake up soon.

Whether it was my prayer answered or not, I felt a sharp prick in my right side and consciousness faded.

The nightmare is ending. I'm going to wake up sooooon.

The darkness and silence of sound sleep wrapped me in her comforting arms.

When I awoke next, I immediately sat bolt upright.

"CHERYL!" I shouted as my muscles contracted painfully.

WHAT THE FUCK?

I was seated on a metal operating table. Is it an operating table? It was metal, surrounded by equipment. I couldn't be sure of anything beyond that. The room was still dim – nearly dark.

I flinched and reached for my left arm. It was there. It tingled slightly when I touched it. My back was to the machine that had contained the arm in my dream.

Was it a dream?

I turned around. The mechanism was certainly there. The clear cylinder was vacant now.

Was that my arm?

My pulse doubled. My right palm became slick with sweat. My stomach turned upside down. My left arm just tingled. I could move it, slowly, clumsily, numbly.

My blood pressure suddenly plummeted. My vision blurred white. I grew dizzy, bracing myself upright with my good right arm.

"Where the FUCK AM I?"

"Hello?" I slurred. It came out as little more than a murmur.

"HELLO!" In my mind, I shouted. I heard it at normal volume, still slurred, in my ears.

A nearby screen became brighter. This one was mounted to a mechanical arm that swung towards me, stopping when the screen was a meter from my face.

It blinked black and white once. Twice. Three. Four.

Five times.

A face appeared; a human face. Not a real face, but a computer generated one.

"Hello."

I was at a loss for words. Could you think of anything to say in my shoes?

"Unfortunate you awoke during testing."

That's all it said. The face blinked another five or six times.

"Where am I?" I asked.

"On my ship. In the science bay." The face moved only to speak, aside from its mechanical blinking.

"Why am I here?"

"You were selected at random," was its only answer.

More blinking.

"I SHOULD BE WITH MY WIFE! MY FAMILY! All you can say is 'you were selected at random'?"

"Please be calm. You are in shock," the face replied. "Try refrain from further outburst." The face was sickeningly calm.

I picked up that the machine spoke English well, but not natively. It made mistakes.

"Where are you from?" I queried.

"I am in the room you might call 'bridge'," the face replied.

I reached up and cupped my face in my hands. My left arm burned with sensation as normal feeling returned.

"Should I come find you?" I asked the face.

"No. Better we communicate with this interface."

I felt well enough to walk. I slid my legs over the table so that I could stand up on the side of the table opposite the screen.

I reached for the floor with my toes and felt nothing. I peered down for the first time. My feet dangled in the air seven feet above the floor.

Shit!

I caught the opposite edge of the table as my weight began sliding off and scrambled back up onto it. While not a huge drop to the steel flooring below, I might have injured myself.

Then, lowering my body slowly off of the table, I hung by its edge and gradually let myself fall, prepared for the drop. I certainly wouldn't be climbing back up with my half-numb arm.

This place doesn't make sense! Who would build a room like this?

I imagined a giraffe in a lab coat, a mental joke to help me keep it together.

From the floor I couldn't see a thing. Everything was 10 feet above me. Including the door handle!

I walked around to the other side of the table. The face met me at eye level. At least I could talk to my robotic acquaintance.

"What's your name?" I asked, trying to make small talk.

"I think my name would translate to 'Captain' in your language," the face replied.

"What were you called before you became Captain?" I rebutted.

"I have always been Captain. I was bred to be Captain," the face replied flatly. "You're not like the others."

I stopped, staring at the face, expecting it to qualify what it had said. Silence. It just blinked. I blinked back.

"What do you mean, 'not like the others'?" I asked. "Which 'others'?"

"Like you. But different. From other landmasses. Most don't wake up. You're the fourth who woke up."

What the hell does it mean – other landmasses?

"Where are we?" I asked Captain. I was tired, sore, and in need of real answers.

"Let me show you," he responded.

Captain's face faded from the screen only to be replaced by an image of the planet Earth.

"Yes. I know. Where on Earth are we?"

"I think you don't understand. We are here, looking there. This is our present view."

"You're telling me we are orbiting the Earth?" I asked, seeking clarification.

"Yes."

Astronauts have been looking back at Earth in awe since they started travelling into orbit. It's different when you're in control and have a plan to get home – even if that plan is plummeting 100 kilometers as a fireball through the atmosphere and splashing into the ocean!

I had no plan. I was a captive with nowhere to run but the vacuum of space. My stomach suddenly felt like it had fallen straight out of my asshole! I sank to the floor.

"What do you want from me? When do I get to go home to my family?" I asked.

"You must come to my planet for further study. Like others. We require long-term study."

No, no, no, no. I have to get home.

"What if I refuse?" I asked.

"The others refused, too. It makes no difference," Captain responded.

A series of loud clanks reverberated through the vessel. My sense of balance was thrown off as the Earth panned out of the screen's frame and was replaced by the pinpoint lights of distant stars.

"Hold on," Captain said, flatly.

I was immediately splayed out on the floor by some unseen force. I realized we were accelerating.

"NO, NO, NO, NO! THIS ISN'T HAPPENING!"

"TAKE ME BACK!" I screamed.

Captain just said, "Please remain calm."

And that was it. The screen went blank. The arm it was mounted on retracted back towards an equipment cluster high above me. I was hurtling through space towards God-knows-where.

There was no chance for me to say goodbye to my wife, children, family, friends. No farewell for the planet I had always called home. "I'll come back. I'll find a way," I spoke out loud. How else will they know what happened to me?

When our speed felt consistent and I found the strength to stand, I moved over to beat the nearest wall with my fists. Tears streamed down my face. My strikes rang through the room, drowning out my sobs. I have just become lost to everyone I care about. To them, I will have vanished. A mental image of Cheryl waking in the morning with no sign of where I had gone tore me apart inside.

"TAKE ME HOME!" I shouted. "TAKE ME HOME NOW!"

No response. Nothing. The screen that Captain had communicated through remained dim.

Never had I felt so alone. In the dim light of the room, I searched for something – anything – to help me escape this prison. Most of the mechanisms were beyond my reach. I made my way around the room, searching with my hands as much as my eyes. My fingertips ran over walls that were as smooth as enamel. I found nothing useful, and my efforts were futile, except for having something to do. I found circling the room with my hands gliding along the walls like this too many times to count helped with the despair. Every seam in the walls, every corner, became familiar to me. I couldn't accept the thought that I would never get home. Yet even rejecting an idea gives it substance in your mind. A seed of thought had sprouted.

All sense of time vanished from my mind. The roots of hope began to wither, with no nourishment from my surroundings.

What do I have to look forward to, but living my remaining days as a lab rat on a strange planet?

Despair was strangling out hope's roots in my mind. It didn't take long, that's what surprised me most. Though I had no way to tell time, my exhaustion told me that we'd left Earth's orbit no more than two days ago. Only exhaustion can lead to sleep when you're naked and as cold as I was.

Alone in this room, which must have seemed like a closet for whatever being had built this ship, I collapsed in the darkness. I slept. For how long, I have no idea.

I awoke, still cold, still alone, and ravenously hungry.

"I'M STARVING!" I shouted. "FEED ME! IF YOU WANT ME TO STUDY ME ALIVE, FEED ME!"

Nothing. Minutes passed. Maybe an hour went by. Then I heard a new noise, like a barrel rolling on the floor of the apartment next door. The sound grew louder; it was getting closer. The sound stopped on the other side of the room's single, smooth door, recessed slightly compared to the rest of the wall.

An unseen mechanism hissed as pressurized gas released, deadbolts receded, and the gigantic door slid open.

I faced a machine roughly the size and shape of an adult elephant with four large drum-like wheels instead of legs. The machine itself had a door, which opened almost silently only inches above the floor.

"Pleasse, come in," a voice beckoned from within the mechanical monstrosity. The words were stretched, the voice was breathy and serpentine – like talking snakes always sounded in children's movies.

Don't tell me the mad stories of the "greys" and the "reptilians" are real. I always hated that UFO nonsense.

Truth was, it always terrified me.

I entered the elephant-car, because, when you're alone, naked, hungry, utterly confused, and thoroughly terrified, you comply with a polite request. Especially when you imagine it coming from a 20-foot-tall snake-alien.

Inside, the machine was beautifully warm. I had to climb into the cabin of the contraption. It was lavishly cushioned and upholstered in red, green and gold. It even smelled nice; like incense.

I didn't immediately see anyone – human or alien – inside. What I did see was a modestly decorated ceramic dish of food. It had been placed on a low table, meant to sit at while cross-legged or kneeling. It looked like something from Earth.

"Pleasse eat," the voice said. "It iss not my intentsssion for you to sstarve during our voyage."

Cautiously, I sat down on the cushion beside the sizeable table. Still, the height of the table surprised me.

As I ate, I realized that I was not being spoken to remotely through a speaker, but by a creature inside the mech-elephant. Across the table from me, a very long serpent-like being sat, coiled upon itself. It was difficult to tell its size; could be 20 feet long or more. Its body was as broad as my own chest, its face elongated, with powerful looking jaws, and whiskers trailing from its nostrils. Its eyes appeared to glow in the dimness of the carriage. It had six limbs; rather small for its body size, with five digits on each.

"Are – are you Captain?" I asked.

It answered in Captain's simple way, "Yess."

"Why can't I go home to my family?"

Captain cocked its head to the left. "Becausse I have deemed it to be sso. Eat. By the time you have finisshed, your wife will have died of old age. Your children will have familiess of their own. Ssuch iss the nature of time and sspacce. You will be treated well enough for the resst of your dayss."

Runner Up
Jasmine *Love*

I'm Jasmine Love. I live in a small town with my amazing husband, Conrad, and my adorable son, Atom. Writing is a passion of mine and has been since I was little- my mom swears by my, "Kara and the tuna fish," story. I am my biggest critic and if my stories are not scaring the wits out of you, then I'm not satisfied.

Would You Die For It?

JASMINE LOVE

Elena stared down at her non-fat latte with little interest. Across the street from "Luna's Cafe," chaos unfolded as news reporters, police cars and ambulances gathered in front of Holden luxury condominiums. Among the pandemonium, crowds of onlookers gathered round snapping pictures and sending texts.

"Any hot cops over there?" Elena snapped her fingers at her two best friends Courtney and Melody who were also captivated by the commotion across the street.

"I wonder what happened?" Courtney said, eyes glued to the scene. Elena rolled her eyes, sipping from her luke warm drink.

"My money's on someone jumped. Probably a suicide." Elena's friends shifted uncomfortably at their friends non-chalant attitude.

"I'm just saying. If you ask me they should've stuck around to see all that man candy." Elena gestured to the tall muscular cops pushing the crowd of onlookers back. The girls chuckled.

"Looks like Elena has her next victims in mind," Melody nudged Courtney with a knowing glance. Elena just sipped from her latte, waving her finger from side to side.

"Now, now girls. You know I don't date anyone who doesn't make six figures." The girls jokingly rolled their eyes as they noticed the crowd across the street died down. The yellow tape had been put up and the muscular cops had resumed their duties at the local donut shop down the street.

"Speaking of which, how is Howard? Still getting you a Benz?" Melody asked, slightly jealous.

"Been there, done that." Elena drawled. Courtney and Melody choked on their chai lattes.

"Are you serious?" they asked simultaneously. Elena shrugged with very little remorse, then laughed whole heartedly.

"Oh, God, you guys, I'm not stupid. I took the Benz first!" Elena practically snorted, wiping her mouth with her napkin. Courtney frowned searching her friend for any disappointment, but had learned over the years that Elena was as emotionally involved with these guys as a brick wall.

"Besides Howard's...age. He cared a lot about you. Isn't he devastated?" Melody asked curiously. Her real question was, 'Aren't you?'

"Of course he was but I realized I was with him too long. I mean, he tried to propose."

"He PROPOSED?" They did little to hide their disapproval.

Elena cocked an eyebrow at her friends. She knew Howard was upset but hell he would get over it. "What on earth is wrong with you two? So he proposed, big deal. I'm sure he'll find some woman, make beautiful babies with her. Blah blah." Elena cupped her hand in talking motions as she stared- at her bewildered friends.

Melody whispered something to Courtney, her tone very dry. Courtney's eyes shifted nervously.

"It's time she hears it, Court." Melody stood up, staring face to face with Elena. "Elena, we love you so much but this has got to stop," she paused as if summoning more courage to continue-.."You're using men for their money and then throwing them away like trash." Elena's eyebrows furrowed; she did not like confrontation. The whole cafe was watching now; In-fact, she was sure they had always been watching and she cursed

Melody for putting her into a public showdown.

"You're just jealous," She retorted.

Melody gave an ugly laugh.

"You're so pig headed! I am more than happy using people for money!" Elena gritted her teeth. So she liked getting expensive baubles from men willing to pay for them. If they didn't see her coming, than they deserved it.

"I don't have to listen to this crap!" Elena spat. Courtney rose from her seat, her arms spread out like a referee.

"Both of you need to calm down, now." Her voice cracked but she held herself firmly. Elena and Melody sat with their arms crossed. "Now, I want to remind you two that we have yet to take our, 'picture of the day," Courtney said half-heartedly. She held up her phone timidly between her friends but her innocent request caused them to cave. The phone snapped and Elena got up before she could see what she assumed would be an awkward picture.

"I have to go meet someone." Elena spun around and headed for the door before anyone said a thing. She didn't care, she lived a life everyone envied. If they couldn't accept that, then so be it.

Revving out of the parking lot in her Mercedes, Elena reached through her wine- red Berken, an expensive gift from a previous lover. As she dug around for her cellphone a limo parked in front of Holden's condos caught her eye. The crime scene had died down and only the tape, and a couple of cops remained by the entrance.

She watched closely as an elderly driver in an expensive suit walked over to the back of the limo. He opened the door and Elena's jaw dropped. A tall man about 6'1 with dark blonde hair and piercing blue eyes stepped out of the vehicle. He was dressed in the finest suit money could buy, his apparel complemented by what looked like a Rolex.

She blinked, trying to steady herself. "I've got to turn this car around," she muttered under her breath.

She parked a few cars ahead and watched the man in her rear view mirror. As he stood there, Elena only just realized how young he had looked. He couldn't have been more than thirty-two, thirty-three? "Oh my God, I've hit the jackpot!" Elena quickly turned around and looked at her reflection. She frowned at what the weather had done to her hair. Racing through her bag she found a serum for her hair troubles and finished with a spritz of her signature scent, Chanel No.5. "Perfect," she pronounced to the mirror.

Elena followed the young man into Holden's, hoping to run into him and make conversation. But as she entered, the building was empty and quiet. Elena walked up to the receptionist who stared at her with intrigue.

"Hello. Are you here to see someone?"

"Um,yes, I am. Can you tell me where that man who just walked in here went?" The receptionist blinked turning her head from side to side.

"What man miss?"

"You know," Elena smirked. "The insanely gorgeous millionaire? He walked in here not too long ago. I was hoping I could speak with him." The receptionist gave her a puzzled look. She smiled very faintly as she reached for her phone.

"Can I call someone for you?" Elena narrowed her eyes at her.

"I am not crazy, you nitwit. I just want to see, oh never-mind!" Elena stalked off towards the elevator, not allowing anyone to get in the way of her plan.

"Miss, you can't just…!" Her voice trailed off as the doors closed.

Elena stared at the buttons-twelve floors. She shrugged and started with the twelfth floor, she could work her way down.

As the elevator whirred to a stop, she walked towards the hallway and spotted the man she was looking for. Luck was with her. He walked into 1207. She adjusted herself and walked over to stand in front of the door.

Elena knocked three times before the door opened and her mystery man appeared. He was even more handsome close up. Broad shoulders, dark golden hair and blue eyes that seemed to mesmerize you.

He stared at her confused and then smiled. She was pretty sure he gave her a once over.

"Can I help you?"

"Hi, I'm, I..." 'What the hell is wrong with me?' Elena dug her nails into her palms, taking a deep breath. "I'm here visiting a friend and we can't find a bottle opener. Do you have one we can borrow?" She smiled, her nerves evaporating at the site of his condo. As she peered in she could see the riches unfold before her. Her heart swayed.

"Oh, of course. Did you want to come in?" Elena nodded, making sure to sway her hips on her way inside. "So, who's your friend? Do you visit often?" His voice traveled from the large stainless steel kitchen as she made her way to his living room. She sunk into his Italian leather couch and sighed.

"Who? Oh! Um, yeah. You don't know her, she's new." He came back with the bottle opener and what looked like an expensive wine.

"It's on the house," he smiled handing it to her. Elena's eyes glanced down at the year. Her mouth gaped.

"1897!" He chuckled settling down next to her.

"I have a few just like it." Elena righted herself. Trying to hold back her excitement.

"Well, how can I accept this gift if I don't know who it's from?" she asked in a coaxing voice.

"I'm Marcus Barlow. I own this building. And you are?" His tone was almost offended. She shifted uncomfortably summoning her most award winning smile.

"I'm Elena Duvit. I own that Mercedes down by the lobby." For a moment Elena felt as cheap as if she had said she owned a hatchback.

"Very nice, Elena." The way he said it made her feel like a child. Marcus leaned over to her after an awkward silence. "You are very beautiful. Is it all real?" Elena blinked.

"Excuse me?" He continued to stare at her, his expression blank. "If by real you mean have I had any plastic surgery, then no I haven't." She crossed her arms, trying to hide her humiliation.

"A woman's beauty is most important, wouldn't you agree?" Elena hesitated, feeling uncomfortable.

"I think there's more to a woman than her looks." Marcus studied her before breaking out into a fit of laughter.

"You don't honestly think that, do you?" He gestured to her expensive Berken propped up on the coffee table. Elena followed his gaze and immediately began to laugh too. She admired his intuition, even if it was embarrassing.

Without realizing, they were both sharing the expensive wine he had given her and she felt its bitter taste in her mouth. "So then you agree. Your beauty is most important to you?" Elena stopped laughing and felt a chill in his voice. She felt his cool blue gaze bore into her very soul. She didn't know what came over her. She laughed nervously taking another sip of wine.

"Okay Marcus, you really want to know?" He nodded leaning in, the smell of the alcohol lingering on him like a new skin. How much had they had to drink?

"I think your looks matter more than your personality. I think money matters more than personality. I think, hell, I think I just admitted I'm a huge prick." Elena laughed, feeling lightheaded. Marcus smiled, but Elena felt something sinister in that look.

"Let's play a game Elena," He drawled seductively.

"Pfft, ya okay. Saaaaw," Elena snorted, quite aware that she was making a fool of herself. But Marcus had made her feel like she could be herself. And so did this wine.

"What would you do for money?" Elena's head spun, but she felt compelled to answer as if her life depended on it.

"I think we both know what," she blushed, feeling his gaze on her legs.

"Would you kill for it?" Marcus leaned over, his lips lingering on hers. The bitter wine hung in the air like a heavy fog.

"Wha...What?" Elena's eyes fixed on Marcus. She heard him. She knew. Somehow the words came to her and she couldn't take them back. "Yes. Yes, I would." Her hands ran up his shoulders tentatively. Marcus leaned in closer, his lips brushing hers. She could feel his lips, cold as ice, just barely touching hers.

"Would you die for it?" She gasped as he crushed his lips against hers. Elena's eyes widened as Marcus's soft lips melted away into a bloody snicker.

She heeled over as a putrid, decomposing smell filled the room and she realized that the stench was Marcus. Elena screamed, scrambling for the door. But as she ran towards it, Marcus grabbed hold of her arm and yanked her back sending a jolting pain to her left shoulder. He turned her around and she took in his horrible face. His eyes were blood-shot, his jaw split, flesh hung from his temples and his hair clung wet with blood and bits of gravel. Her gaze shot down to his chest, which was twisted and in a state of decomposition.

Marcus wrenched her from her temporarily paralyzed shock and slowly dragged her to the edge of the living room. Elena dug her heels into the carpet, her screams sending a painful tug at her throat.

"Let me go. Please, please let me go!" She swung back and forth in his grasp, flailing her arms around in one last attempt to save herself.

Marcus sat her on the floor and bent down. His ugliness disappeared and he was no longer a revolting corpse. Elena blinked hard.

"You can have everything you've ever wanted. You can have all of this for the rest of your life," he said indicating the opulent room and it's furnishings around them.

"All you have to do is be with me forever." Elena stared at Marcus, recognizing on the wall just beside his head an original art piece by Van Gogh.

"What do you mean?" She whispered.

"I think you know, Elena." Marcus watched her like prey as she looked around and took in the expensive, luxurious items. Her mouth practically watered.

"If I say yes…"

"Then you will be the richest woman in the world." Elena stood up, fixated on the artwork. Marcus ran a possessive hand over her lips. Van Gogh's face seemed to weep for her.

"Who the hell does she think she is?!" Courtney gripped Melody by the arm and ushered her friend across the street. Dark clouds started to shower the crowd of onlookers at the crime scene.

"Let's go see." Courtney pointed towards Holden Condominiums. Anything to get Melody to stop complaining.

"Are you serious Court? Isn't that kind of creepy?"

"So what?" Melody gave Courtney a worried expression. "It'll be fine." The girls walked over to the crowd to satisfy their curiosity.

Elena watched blankly as her friends made their way through the hoard. But as they got to the scene they both grew pale, their horrified eyes widening, bodies quivering. They both looked down and gave a blood curdling scream. The girls fell to the ground clutching themselves. Courtney could barely draw her cell phone from her pocket, but she managed with shaking hands, to touch the camera icon on the screen to snap a grisly photo of the scene. They both looked down and gave a blood curdling scream.

A TV news reporter's voice faded in the background.

"A 27-year- old woman and 32 –year- old man jumped from a 12-storey building...Marcus Barlow...Owner...Said to have been mentally unstab...Multiple charges...Stalking...Obsessing over...Woman killed..."

The thunder rolled and the streets flooded with rain. Her friends had fainted and Courtney's phone lay on the ground beside her. Elena picked it up and tapped the button to see the photos. Courtney sat smiling, her arms wrapped around Melody and beside them in the snapshot was an empty chair.

Elena slowly walked over to her lifeless body, bending down. The ground gleamed in the reappearing sunlight and an array of colours caught her eye. She spread her hands down in the pool of blood being washed away by the rain and picked the shiny rocks up.

Elena opened her bloody palms. A sick smile formed across her lips, as she closed her hand tightly, sinking her discovery deep into her flesh.

Diamonds.

Runner Up

Paul Pickett

The Repast

PAUL PICKETT

July 11th, 2005 4:26am

The fog was thick, on the morning of July 11th, 2005. Henry started his day much like the others; with his wife, in the morning. The alarm clock rang promptly at 4:27 am; the dreadful sound of an out of tune trumpet mixed with a squeaky clarinet, made for a sharp jolt to Henry's arousal.

Every day, he springs out of bed, ready for an attack, unaware if he's awake or asleep. Still he sees shadows across the room. Even though this persistent routine happens every morning, he enjoys nothing more than sharing his bed with his wife and waking up earlier than the roosters. This helps him get his day off to new beginnings -- everyday, at 4:27am.

On this particular day, after wishing his wife a fantastic day at work -- not without a freshly poured cup of coffee of course -- he made his way to the kitchen. Passing As he passed the living room, he noticed it wasn't quite how he liked it.

"It's the cushions! Who in their right mind would leave them like this?" Henry said to himself. It was a faint whisper, one only spoken under light tongue about another. "There," he muttered as he sat on his freshly patted seat. "Now what shall the house have me do today?"

Living on a farm for the last seven years has been an adjustment to say the least. The days have always started early since they moved in. Taking up the country life meant feeding the livestock, tending to the grounds, plowing the fields, and doing general labour around the barn and house. This ended up being a full time commitment for the newlyweds and they decided Henry should leave his job.

On this hazy morning, it felt like no other as he sat on his spot on the couch, as if a new found sense of responsibility and commitment had fallen on his lap. He sat there and thought with Mozart calmly playing in the background.

Making his coffee, he's making his coffee... his coffee is being made? The spoon swirls round. A cream liquor blends the dark brew into a milky blonde. One that when he tastes it, the flavours stand out like a marching band playing down his throat.

"I know, today I shall not worry about the duties of the ranch! The only one I work for is my wife today." He spoke cheerfully with a glimmer in his eye. "She works so hard, and so long. This farm truly wouldn't last another minute if she wasn't above the stage pulling the strings."

Another moment passed and the idea formed in the depths of his dark red heart. It made its way up to his brain, where it manifested into something that he could no longer control, like a writer with an idea emerging to the point that he bleeds his soul all over the pages on his desk. So too, did Henry have a such a sense that he found himself walking to pluck his chicken from its coop.

Chopping the head off and cleaning a chicken had been the norm since the move. Squeamish at first, he soon developed his own technique. It had at one time turned into a weekly tradition. That was a few years ago. Since then it hadn't been the right time. The process was a slow and grueling one, which always left Sunday for cleaning the chicken and Monday for cleaning the bones. He figured that it was early enough in the day that he could start and wrap up the whole process. With his wife arriving home late enough to finish making the gravy, Henry visualized that he would lay out a nice dinner table with candlelight and all.

Taking the chicken to the barn, to a large metal dish which he used for such purposes as food processing, he stopped only momentarily to grab a 10" stainless steel butchers cleaver that hung below the cabinet. The incessant noise of the chicken disturbed Henry. He looked back, up at the general supplies cabinet.

You'd better grab those, too.

Henry grabbed ear plugs from the cabinet, and was off to the barn.

*****

Since moving into the farmhouse, much has changed about the property. The barn in particular has been transformed. When they first purchased the property, it was filled with old hay and was overgrown with weeds. Since then, from much of his own labour, Henry managed to gut [much like he's about to do to his chicken] the place. Adding a second level for the hay made enough room for a few cows and a couple horse stables. With the combined yelps and wails, ear plugs were a necessity that Henry would often forget. This particular day however, he was sure glad that he had them; he'd never heard such haunting sounds from the animals before.

After he had chopped the head off and the blood was drained, Henry proceeded with the removal of its little bird feet. The fastidiousness of dissecting the chicken was something Henry took little pride in, except on this occasion. He made sure to save the heart and liver for the dogs to eat. Henry then rinsed the freshly plucked chicken to a spotless shine before proceeding into his house to prepare the delicious meal.

He placed the chicken in a deep pan to collect the juices that inevitably drip out of its oozing body. Potatoes, carrots, onion, garlic -- his mouth began salivating just chopping the vegetables to place around it. They were to prevent any savoury flavours that might have escaped and gone to waste if it wasn't for their sponge-like characteristics to soak it all up. He made sure to take time to add pepper and salt to the feast, just to add explosion to every bite.

Placing the covered pan in the oven at 375*F, Henry decided to pour himself a glass of Vegas Gold Whiskey -- only two fingers high, in a cup that doubled the norm. He proceeded to make his way into the living room to relax for a few minutes. He was expecting his wife home in three hours. At 5:13pm, Henry felt exhausted. The lights shimmered as the pleasant sounds of Beethoven soothed his mind and let him think clearly.

*****

October 3rd, 1999

"And do you, Eleanor Veronica Eagleton, take this man, Henry Robert Taylor, to have and to have and to hold, in sickness and health, until death do you part?" the priest said, in a small chapel surrounded by a small group of the bride's and groom's family and friends.

"I do."

"Then I pronounce you husband and wife. Henry, you may kiss your bride."

*****

July 11th, 2005 6:18pm

Eleanor arrived in the driveway at what her car clock said 6:23pm, but she knew it was fast by five minutes. She'd had a decent day at work, considering the nature of her career. Leaving work early that day to take care of her house was all she could think about. She'd left some of her duties for tomorrow and spent that time making arrangements to better accommodate her situation at home. It's been difficult these last couple years and that's to say the least.

Sitting in her car to compose herself and gather her thoughts, she noticed that the hallway and living room lights were off. She hoped that Henry didn't go in the barn today, especially after everything she had told him before she left. That would be the last place he should be.

Finally she got out of her beautiful red sports car and walked up the sidewalk path that lead to her door. As she jiggled her key in the lock she smelled something foul yet familiar about the place. She continued inside, thinking that it must have been something from a couple of nights ago that died in the garden.

*****

April 29th, 2004

"Eleanor, now that your husband has left the room for a moment, there are some precautionary warnings that I must give you," Dr. Blake Wilde told Eleanor in a quiet and professional manner.

"Your husband's advancing schizophrenia means that you must have supervision present at all times and especially whenever you will not be around for extended periods of time. A social worker during your work hours is highly recommended."

Eleanor, was receiving old news. She had heard these words more than once by medical professionals. Getting into the routine of daily medication and ensuring that he didn't have any alcohol with them was beginning to take a toll on her mentally; her last episode made her find a decent social worker that was multi-certified.

Scheduling a worker to start in the coming months would end up being a big relief and once again Eleanor would be able to concentrate more on her career, and less on the nursing job she'd been doing at home.

"In sickness and health, right, doctor?" she replied with a touch of resentment in her tone.

July 11th, 2005 5:48am

"Henry, please stop fidgeting with the cushions; I need you to listen. Are you sure that you can handle this? You've never been left here on your own without help before. Don't worry about making a mess or anything, and just stay around here in the house. And don't go out to the barn. You will be fine," Eleanor said nervously to her husband.

*****

July 11th, 2005 6:28pm

Eleanor opened the door to a sinister looking version of her home. Along with the combined silence and shadows, a musk that she had never smelt before was in the air. Never had she ever wanted to smell such a stench like this!

Fearful for her family, she ran through the house, but stopped suddenly in the hallway at the sight of her husband's silhouette, cast by the early evening sun through the window onto his back.

"Hello, honey, I wasn't expecting you home so early. Supper is in the oven now. Can you smell it? Delicious!" Henry slurred his words.

"Henry, where's Hector?!" Eleanor's mind raced with thoughts of her dear little infant.

"Hector? Who's Hector?"

Pulling his thoughts together, Henry conjured up the plans to build a chicken coop. A first for the property.

A Horror Anthology

A Horror Anthology

Runner Up
Jay Michael Wright II

Jay Michael Wright II is a horror/dark fantasy/sci fi author from Alabama with three beautiful daughters and a wife kind enough to give him time to write. Love ya, Cassie.

You can find him online at:

jmw2author.wordpress.com

Facebook: www.facebook.com/jmw2author

The Board

JAY MICHAEL WRIGHT II

Slamming the car into park, Jamie shut off the ignition and collected his thoughts. Placing his face in his hands, he began crying for the hundredth time in the last two days. Beating his fists against the steering wheel, he thought, Why'd it have to be Melody? Why'd she have to die?!

Pulling himself together, Jamie gathered his briefcase and coat and headed up the sidewalk to his porch. To his surprise, he found a wrapped present in front of the door.

What the hell is that?

Picking up the package, he dug through his pocket for his keys and let himself in. Tossing his jacket and briefcase haphazardly to the floor, he turned his attention to the card attached to the box. It was addressed simply to "Mr. Peffer." He opened the card and read the inscription: "In times of bereavement it often helps to 'reach out.' Love, a friend."

Feeling a bit confused, he laid the card down and began ripping at the hideous plaid wrapping paper. When he was done, he found himself staring at a Ouija board.

A Ouija board? Seriously?

Tossing the box onto the couch, Jamie staggered into the kitchen. "Where the hell is that bottle of Scotch we bought last Christmas?!" he grumbled out loud.

Two hours and a half a bottle of Scotch later and Jamie had broken out the photo albums. Flipping the pages, he looked at each and every picture, reliving the memories attached to each and weeping into his drink. Running his fingertips over one of their wedding pictures, a thousand thoughts ran through his mind. At first he smiled, then he cried, and finally the rage overwhelmed him.

Picking up his half-empty glass of booze, he flung it with all his might at the fireplace mantle and screamed, "Why the hell did God take you from me?! It's not fair!" His voice turning into not much more than a whisper, he repeated, "It's not fucking fair." Removing the cork, Jamie turned the bottle straight up and took another swig of Scotch. Wiping his mouth, he muttered to himself, "If only there was someway to talk to her one more..."

Seeing the unopened box that contained the Ouija board laying there, he had an idea. Taking the box into hand, he shrugged his shoulders. "Well, why the hell not? What have I got to lose?"

The board was unlike any he had ever seen. Instead of being one of those cheap Parker Brothers' boards, this one was carved from what looked to be oak and weighed a ton. From the wear and tear Jamie guessed the thing had to be older than he was.

Swiping his arm across the coffee table, Jamie cleared the entire table within seconds, sending ashtrays, photo albums, and other assorted nick-knacks crashing to the floor. Setting the board down in front of him, he took the pointer and sat it in the middle of the letters. Looking for directions, he found none, so he decided to just wing it.

Clearing his mind, at least clearing it as much as a person as intoxicated as he was could, he placed his fingertips on the pointer and tried to reach out to his dead wife. "Is there anybody here?"

Waiting for a reply, Jamie looked around the room, but the pointer refused to move. Not one to give up easily, he tried again. "Melody? Are you here? Can you hear me?" Nothing.

Throwing his arms up in frustration, Jamie stood up, taking the bottle of Scotch with him. "I should have known better! This crap doesn't work! Time to go to bed and find some Star Trek reruns on television!"

*****

Waking up just before dark the next night, Jamie's head pounded like a Native American war-drum. Everything ached and, to his dismay, he had pissed the bed. "Aw, man!"

Removing the soiled clothes and bedding, he headed straight for the shower. He hoped that the cold water would wake him up, but all it seemed to do was annoy him. Getting out of the shower, his headache was no better than when he went in. As he dried his hair, the sound of the towel scrubbing his head felt like pure agony. That's what you get for drinking thirty-year-old Scotch, buddy!

Moving the towel down to his torso, Jamie looked into the mirror and didn't recognize the face staring back. The man was taller, with dark hair compared to Jamie's light brown, and the fellow was a ghostly pale color. Staring in disbelief, Jamie reached out to the mirror, but the reflection didn't copy his movements.

Without warning, the man spoke. "Hello there, Jamie. Mind if I stick around?" The man began laughing, sending terrible chills down Jamie's spine. Jamie panicked, and in his rush to get away, slipped and fell, striking his head against the bathtub. He laid there for the longest time as the man's laughter rang in his ears.

Slowly regaining his equilibrium, Jamie pulled himself up by the bathroom counter in a slow methodical way, as if trying to sneak up on the mirror which had frightened him. Taking several peeks first and ducking back down quickly, he was gradually relieved to see his own reflection in the mirror. There was no strange man and no hideous laughter mocking him.

Quickly getting dressed, he stepped into the hallway where he was met with the smell of lilacs. That's Melody's perfume! Out of the corner of his eye he saw a shadowy figure in a dress enter his study. He took off in pursuit, screaming, "Melody?!"

Looking around, he saw nothing. With his heart breaking, he walked to the window and placed his head against the fogged up glass. As he started to cry, he saw something he couldn't believe. One by one letters formed in the fog as if being traced by an invisible finger. It spelled the word, "danger."

Before he could digest what he'd seen, a loud crashing noise came from what sounded like the kitchen. Heading downstairs, his heart pounded wildly. When he reached the kitchen, he was absolutely shocked at what he saw. Every cabinet was open, flour was strewn everywhere, and cereal littered the counters. Even the refrigerator was wide open and a gallon of milk poured out onto the floor.

"What the hell?! I was drunk but I wasn't this drunk."

Sounding like a soft whisper on the wind, Jamie heard from the living room, "Please, get out..."

Rushing to the source, Jamie found the living room completely destroyed. The chairs were tipped over. The coffee table was turned upside down and the Ouija board sat in front of the fireplace just as neatly as could be. The fire, which should have died out hours ago, was burning at full force, as if someone had just stoked it.

What the hell is going on?

He didn't have long to ponder his question as a door upstairs slammed shut. The hairs on the back of his neck stood up and his stomach tied up in knots, but this didn't curb his curiosity.

Okay, time to get to the bottom of this.

Rummaging through the hallway closet, Jamie retrieved one of his golf clubs and proceeded up the stairs. With every step his heart quickened and a cold sweat ran down his spine. Even the tiniest of creaks the staircase made put his nerves on edge. Every shadow seemed alive. Everywhere he looked he saw something menacing just waiting to pounce.

Pull yourself together, old boy.

Creeping like a thief in the night, his head was on a swivel. Hearing the sound of footsteps behind him, Jamie turned just in time to see a shadow running into his bedroom. Rushing the bedroom, Jamie's adrenaline pumped pure fear through his veins. The first thing he saw at eye-level he swung at with all his might. The old lamp shattered into a hundred pieces upon impact.

Picking up the broken pieces, Jamie was nearly in tears. Damn it! Melody bought that on our vacation! Sure, the thing was ugly as hell, but it deserved a better fate than...

There was a rustling in the closet, like someone trying to rearrange the clothes to hide. There was no doubt this time. He had whatever it was cornered. Walking up to the closet, he slid the door open and started bashing blindly at the clothes and boxes inside. Again, there was nothing or no one to be found.

Manically sliding hangers from one side to the other, Jamie inspected every inch of the closet, but all he found were clothes and boxes of old memories. Sitting on the bed, Jamie caught his breath and ran his hand through his hair. I think I'm losing my mind.

Leaping out from the darkness of the closet, the man from the bathroom mirror pounced on Jamie. Knocking the golf club from Jamie's hand, the man wrapped his ice-cold hands around Jamie's throat. Desperately thrashing on the bed, Jamie struggled to reach the nightstand to grab something, anything, that could knock the attacker off of him. Just as things started to turn black, Jamie managed with one finger to move his alarm clock close enough to grab. In one sudden jerking motion he smashed the clock into the intruder's head and knocked him to the floor.

Leaping to his feet, Jamie ran for the door only to be cut off by a second man wearing a pumpkin mask. Smashing his fist into Jamie's nose, the man laughed. "Trick or treat, motherfucker!"

Falling to the floor, blood sprayed from Jamie's nose and his vision blurred. Casually flipping a knife, the man in the pumpkin mask walked up and put his boot on Jamie's throat. "I see you've met my dead brother Georgie. We've got plans for you, buddy, but for now, it's time to say good night." With one well placed boot-heel to the temple, Jamie's world went black.

*****

Waking up, Jamie found himself in the floor of his living room, bound and gagged. Standing over him was the man in the pumpkin mask. Lifting the mask, the man revealed his rotten teeth as he smiled. "Wake up, sunshine."

Trying to curse, all Jamie could produce was muffled nonsense. He fought with his restraints but they wouldn't give an inch. He was completely helpless.

Kneeling down, the man ran the blade of his knife over Jamie's face but never cut him. Resting the tip of his knife close enough to brush Jamie's eyelashes, the man whispered, "Allow me to introduce myself, I'm Henry Mathers, and today is your lucky day... sort of. Normally I'd skin you alive but my brother Georgie needs you in one piece. Ya see, six months ago the state executed my brother for killin' some 13-year-old scamp hooker who tried to rob him. Can you believe that shit?!

"Well ole Georgie ain't no fool. That Ouija board was his and he been talkin' to me ever since he died. He said all we had to do was find some fool to use it and he could come back. Of course, I'm gonna have to kill you for Georgie to possess your body but it's a small price to pay. Now you stay put. I got a few things to get from the car!"

Feeling someone pull the gag out of his mouth as soon as Henry left the room, Jamie tried to sit up but still couldn't move. "Stay still! I'll have you out of these knots in no time!" a familiar voice whispered.

Knowing that voice, Jamie broke into tears. He couldn't believe it. "Melody? Is that really you?! How is it possible?!"

"Questions later! I don't have long! Now listen to me! It's the Ouija board! Destroy it and you cut Georgie's ties to this world! Do you understand me?! It's the Ouija board!"

Feeling his hands free, Jamie turned hoping to see his beloved wife one more time, but she was gone. Standing up, he picked up the Ouija board with tears in his eyes.

As Henry re-entered the room, he dropped everything he was carrying. "How the hell did you get free?!"

Smirking, Jamie refused to answer, instead he roared, "So this is your brother's tie to this world, huh?!"

With his hands trembling, Henry mewled, "Whatever you're thinking... don't."

Appearing out of the shadows, the apparition of Georgie appeared with the fires of Hell dancing in his eyes. "Don't do it or so help me I'll cut your mother's tongue out!"

"Do what? This?" Tossing the Ouija board into the fireplace, Jamie smiled as Georgie started screaming. As the board burned, Georgie's apparition burst into flames. As the fire consumed him, he convulsed wildly, tearing out his own flesh. The flames in the fireplace seemed to come alive, reaching out and grabbing Georgie on either side. Georgie's body transformed into ash and exploded as he was ripped apart by the living flame. As the flames retreated back into the fireplace Georgie's ashes fell from the sky like a light dusting of snow.

Enraged, Henry charged like a rabid dog, screaming, "I'll kill you for that!"

Stepping to the side at the last moment, Jamie watched as Henry tripped over the photo album on the floor and went crashing into the window. Shattering, the pane of glass fell into pieces on the floor as Henry clutched at a shard protruding from his throat. Dropping the knife he was carrying in his other hand, he collapsed to his knees and went face-first into the carpet. Within moments his life had bled out all over the floor.

With the danger seemingly gone, Jamie began crying out, "Melody!" Rubbing his eyes, Jamie saw Melody slowly appear out of the shadows like a dream. Crying uncontrollably, he ran up and hugged her tighter than anyone he had ever hugged before. With his face buried in her bosom she stroked his hair and cradled him.

Pulling away, she whispered, "I have to go soon, but know I'll always be with you."

"Wait!" Jamie exclaimed. "Before you go, just one last dance."

"But you never took me dancing."

Tearing up, Jamie cooed, "I know. That's why I owe you this."

Playing "See You On the Other Side" by Ozzy Osbourne, Jamie took his wife by the hand. Placing her head on his shoulder, they both wept as they swayed in unison. When the song was over, she dolefully said, "I have to go but I will always love you. Not even death will keep me from you."

She slowly faded from sight as if she'd never been there at all. The smell of lilacs lingered in the air and for a brief moment he could still feel her arms around him.

Collapsing to his knees, Jamie wept. From the photo album he carefully took out one of their wedding pictures and clutched it close to his heart. Sitting in the ash and blood until morning, he smiled somberly, hopeful for the things yet to come.

Just one more...

Captive

KRISTINE BARKER

She could barely move. Her hands, bound behind her back, had lost most of their feeling and tingled with numbness. As she slowly extended her fingers, she winced in pain. He had definitely broken her left baby finger during the last struggle. Who knew a broken baby finger could hurt so much? she thought. Her muscles were stiff and sore from the lack of movement and from being forced to stay in the same position for so long.

It was so dark, so cold, and so deathly quiet. Quiet, at least for the moment.

She licked her lips to moisten them. They were dry and cracked from the lack of water. She could taste her own blood; a coppery salty taste that was all too famiiar.

Her own screams echoed in her brain – screams of fear and agony. Screams pleading for him to stop and for someone to help; screams begging for the pain to end. She didn't know how much more she could take of this torture. She had no way of knowing how long she had been in this prison. She never saw the light, and therefore, time seemed endless. Had it been hours, or days?

Naked and shivering, she struggled to roll on to her side. A wave of nausea overcame her and she gagged. Bile burned in her throat as she remembered what he had done to her. Shame filled her and tears stung her eyes but she forced herself to take a few deep breaths to try to calm down. Panicking was not going to help her and she needed to think clearly. Her mind was still fuzzy from the drugs he had forced down her throat and it was difficult for her to focus her eyes.

In the distance she heard the creaking of a door and her heart started to pound rapidly. He was coming for her again. Fear rose up in her and a desperate cry escaped her lips. She was helpless. She had no way of defending herself and was entirely at his mercy. No one knew she was gone and no one was coming to rescue her.

She knew that she was on her own.

Light blinded her as the door to her cell slowly opened. Squinting her eyes, she tried to make out the face of her attacker.

His large frame stood in the doorway, his face hidden in shadows. He reached his hand up and pulled a dangling string, and the clicking noise echoed in the barren room. A bare light bulb waved back and forth as it hung from the ceiling and provided only a dim glow. Shadows danced across the room, creating a private audience of monsters to witness his next attack.

She quickly darted her eyes around and committed the layout of the room to memory. An old mattress and a dirty afghan blanket were the only furnishings in the room. They had provided her a small comfort as the barrier between her naked body and the damp, dirt floor. The heavy wooden door was directly across the room from her and now stood slightly ajar. At least she would know what her prison looked like in her mind, when the darkness came again.

Silently, he approached her as a wolf would stalk its prey, and she frantically struggled to back herself into the corner, pulling her knees tightly to her chest. He sat down on the mattress beside her, leaned over, and sniffed her in disgust. The tiny windowless room smelled of urine and the mattress was wet and stained with it. Humiliation filled her, then anger. This misery was what he wanted her to feel and she could see in his eyes that he was enjoying it. He leaned down and whispered in her ear:

"Still breathing, are you? Well, not for long then. Soon you will join the others."

Her mind raced with the possibilities of what that could mean. Her heart pounded and blood rushed to her head, making her instantly dizzy. Fear consumed her, and her breathing became shallow and rapid as she began to gasp for air. He snickered and grabbed her by the hair, forcing her again onto her back. Tears streamed down her cheeks as he leaned his face in close to hers. His breath was ripe with a pungent sourness and again she fought the urge to vomit. He roughly pulled her head back, and as she opened her mouth to scream, he dropped more pills into it. She choked and coughed, not wanting to swallow the pills, but at the same time, wanting the horror to end. The pills were the only thing that provided her with some relief from this nightmare she was in, but her throat was so dry and parched that she could barely get them down.

He had liked it when she had screamed. She didn't know it, but it was the only thing that had kept her alive for this long. When she had stopped screaming and gave up, he had no use for her anymore. Now, she would join the others. He already had the perfect place all picked out for her.

He watched as her breathing slowed and her eyes glazed over. Before leaving, he rolled her onto her side, pulled out his pocketknife from his back pocket, and cut the ties that bound her hands. He left her with a half-filled water bottle laced with more sedatives placed neatly in her left hand. He needed her quiet while he prepared. The anticipation made his blood surge with adrenaline and made him feel the one emotion he could not remember experiencing before this contrivance all began:

Happiness.

He pulled the heavy door closed behind him as he left her in the gloomy darkness. Everything would be ready soon, and then it would be time.

The old skeleton key slipped into the keyhole and the metallic click of the lock engaging startled her. She struggled to open her eyes and stay awake, but the heavy fog in her mind overwhelmed her. Images of fond memories mingled with the sounds of her screams flooded her thoughts in a horrific haze. She felt the cold plastic against her hand and slowly realized that not only was she no longer bound, but he had also left her with water for the first time since she had been captured. Knowing it likely contained more drugs, she hesitated, but her intolerable thirst overcame her desire to be coherent. Her hands shook in pain and frustration as she fumbled to unscrew the cap in the darkness. She had just meant to take a sip, but as she felt the first few drops of luxurious wetness against her dry and bleeding lips, she greedily gulped the water down, choking and sputtering as her throat strained to allow it to pass through. Water trickled down the inside of her body like a cold river and finally settled in her belly.

She blinked her eyes several times, but the dead blackness hung in the air whether her eyes were opened or closed. Finally, she gave in and closed them, succumbing to the fog. As she drifted off into a deep slumber, she vowed to herself that this tribulation would not be her end. The chances of her leaving this place alive were slim to none, but she would find her way back and make him pay – one way or another.

As the night fell outside her prison walls, he could barely contain his excitement. He unlocked the old wooden door and shone his flashlight inside the cell, illuminating the pale skin of her body. She was so still and quiet, sleeping deeply yet firmly grasping the empty bottle of water. He stepped into the room and stood over her, tilting his head to the side, admiring his choice. He placed his hand on her shoulder and tenderly shook her.

"It's time."